Delusion

Lucy's Breath

By Jerry Bader

Copyright © 2019 Jerry Bader

ISBN Paperback: 978-1-988647-65-4

Hard Cover: 978-1-988647-66-1

Ebook: 978-1-988647-67-8

HARRY AND HARRIET

Preamble

On a chilly November New York City morning in 1953, a scientist working for the CIA on psychotropic mind-control experiments walked off the tenth-floor balcony of the Statler Hotel. He had become increasingly disenchanted with the bizarre and incredibly dangerous work he had been doing in service to national security.

Despite the patriotic rationale, the scientist felt his life's work was immoral and most certainly illegal. He wanted out, unfortunately, he knew too much, and knowing too much is a very precarious position to be in if you work for a clandestine operation run by America's very own version of Josef Mengele, the Angel of Death.

The scientist insisted on getting out, and out he got, through the window and off the balcony of the Statler Hotel on that brisk Fall morning in Manhattan. Was suicide his solution for terminating his deal with the devil or did the devil do him in? It's impossible to say. The evidence although in plain sight is murky and blurred by time and the self-preservation of those responsible.

I know what you're thinking, not in my America, not in my beloved United States, not in the home of the brave and the land of the free. Unfortunately, it did happen; it's the kind of thing that happens when governments feel an existential threat.

America has a fundamental flaw, an Achilles heel of perspective and attitude; it fails to understand history and its place in it. In the words of philosopher, George Santayana, "Those who cannot remember the past are condemned to repeat it."

If you believe it can't happen here, I urge you to take a look at The Wall Street Putsch of 1933, and the name of one of the participants. You might find it informative. It could happen again. America is under siege by a series of existential threats. It's not some crackpot conspiracy theory; it's history. The question I have is: which is more dangerous, the external threat or the internal threat?

For those who cling to Senator Barry Goldwater's Cold War aphorism, "Extremism in defence of liberty is no vice." I urge you to remember the past because if you don't, you will be condemned to a future you did not expect and an existence you will be forced to endure.

What follows could happen, and maybe will happen if you allow extremism to take hold of the levers of power.

Prologue

Present Day

It was a beautiful day, the kind of day that almost demands you go for a walk, and so Morton Bigelow, Secretary of State, strolled into the wooded hills near Thurmont, Maryland, on the grounds of Camp David.

The previous evening a dinner was held for a select group of Cabinet Secretaries, White House advisors, senior military men, and their spouses. The affair was hosted by Vice President Leonard Bowater and his wife, Pijiu Brewery scion Barbara Pijiu Bowater. Also present at the party was the other half of the Pijiu billions, Barbara's younger sister, Gloria Pijiu Blackburn, wife of Malcolm Blackburn, CEO of Blackburn Security. Attorney General, Stephen Douglas Marcel, and his artist wife, Anna, were also part of the group.

The dinner was billed as a birthday celebration for the Secretary of State. Navy cooks prepared special dishes for the guests while Malcolm Blackburn supplied supplemental security, including two ex-Navy Seals wearing suits with eight-hundred dollar black Fendi sneakers.

Lurking in the corner of the kitchen was a bizarre little man in a rumbled suit. The civilian had a noticeable limp due to a birth defect that caused one foot to be shorter than the other. The man was not identified. He wore no security badge or any official credentials. If anyone asked who he was, the Secret Service Agent in-charge told them, he wasn't there.

After dinner, the spouses retreated to an entertainment area where they drank Hine Antique Cognac, talked, and played bridge. Special coffees and desserts where served. Rumour had it, the gathering became quite animated with some suggestion the party deteriorated into an ego-fuelled experiment in self-indulgence, unusual for public figures normally careful to keep their excesses under-wraps.

Meanwhile, the power brokers gathered in a meeting room where they drank and argued over reports concerning the obscure and formally non-existent *Lucy's Breath* program: a CIA initiative that some claimed was MK Ultra reborn: an experimental mind-control program with a dodgy history of hazardous illegal experiments. Some reports claim several Cabinet members almost came to blows. The shabby man with a limp remained close at hand in the shadows.

The next morning, Bigalow's body was found hanging from a tree in the idyllic woods of Maryland. But that was not the only unfortunate incident that befell the guests of the previous evening's unconventional event.

The wife of the Attorney General, Anna Marcel, wrapped her brand new Cadillac Escalade around an expansive White Oak. Despite a substantial contusion on her head, she managed to seemingly escape the incident without permanent damage.

Although Marcel's husband was scheduled to drive back to Georgetown with his wife, he decided to hop a ride back to Washington on a helicopter with James K. Delaney, Director of National Intelligence. There were things raised at the party that Marcel felt he needed to discuss with Delaney.

Over the next few weeks, an epidemic of bizarre accidents, illnesses, and strange behaviour befell several of the guests who attended the party. The Attorney General fell down a flight of stairs shattering his pelvis and injuring his head; leaving him more than a little dazed and confused. The Director of National Intelligence had a mental breakdown and was stashed in an isolation ward at Walter Reed National Military Medical Center.

The Secretary of State was replaced by General William Armstrong, CJCS, while the DNI's role was taken by Admiral Thomas MacMullen, VCJCS. Attorney General Marcel was replaced by the President's personal lawyer and longtime friend, retired Marine Colonel, David C. Carmichael.

There are those in government that are not happy with the composition and direction of the new Cabinet and the appointments of senior Presidential advisors. Bigelow, Delaney, and Marcel were all concerned with the *Lucy's Breath* initiative and the continued militarization of the executive branch. Marcel made the mistake of sharing his concerns with his wife.

Harry's Broom Closet

I'm lucky I didn't end up in Her Majesty's Prison, Belmarsh, locked away in an isolation cell so that I couldn't corrupt the various murders, rapists, and sundry other evil-doers with my vivid imagination and interest in abstract expressionism.

Instead, my reward for uncovering a plot to corrupt the Canadian elections and push the Western alliance further to the right was to be exiled to a former broom closet in the basement of the British Consulate in Toronto. You may ask why would someone who just saved Western democracy from further rot be sentenced to obscurity in a former utility room?

The fact is, I was already red-circled and labeled mad as a hatter by the Top Floor. And that was before I met Harriet, who may or may not exist; and before I killed my mechanic and his hitman sidekick. However, I really do feel I was justified; after all, Freddy, my mechanic, and his henchman did try to kill me twice, and he was *The Beautiful Rat*, leader of the local *Sister Project* whose mission was to fix the Canuck election. But of course, you know all this already because I've related the details of the episode to you some time ago in an exhaustive, if somewhat meandering, memo.

No... the sin that got be banished to my very own Muldar-style basement dungeon was planting evidence in the form of my boss's, extravagantly expensive Graf von Faber-Castell fountain pen at the murder scene when I burned down Freddy's garage with Freddy and his pal in it; not that they cared at that point because they had both passed on to that great spy network in the sky due to an extreme case of lead poisoning inflicted by me with Freddy's very own semi-automatic Beretta.

On the other hand, Professor Roger Ames, Psy.D, my boss, the very man I set up to take the fall for the murders, because I believed and still do, that he was the inside mole for Freddy's group of treasonous bastards, was instead rewarded with the top job on the Top Floor. Good old Roger, the hero of the *Sister Project* business was MI6's brand spanking new Kim Philby wannabe, at least, in my humble opinion.

And that brings us to Harriet, aah Harriet, the girl every man still able to perform without the aid of a pharmacological enhancement would want to bed, that is of course if she actually exists; a fact that has always been in question both by me and my boss, Roger. I am a man of reason, facts, and evidence but if truth be told I am open to the possibility that lovely Harriet is merely the

clever self-induced manipulation of some dys-
functional grey matter gone astray. I want to believe she exists; I can still taste the slight trickle
of blood she was fond of inflicting when she
kissed me.

Roger said she is a figment of my imagination, a
fanciful case of delusional transfer associated
with a female advertising spokesperson that
dominated every conceivable marketing medium
from billboard to television for over a year.

I had to admit the possibility of the confusion; I
do have an active imagination and a hopefully
benign case of Pareidolia that normally only
manifests itself in me seeing faces in the abstract
expressionist paintings I collect. The evidence
seemed to point to a creative mental fabrication
since once the advertising queen disappeared
from the scene, replaced by a less pleasing version, so did Harriet.

That being said, I do miss her, whether she is real
or not. However, there is hope; a small notice ap-
peared in one of my newspapers, announcing the
former advertising it-girl was rewarded for her
hawking efforts with a new dramatic series on
cable. The promise of a major marketing campaign featuring the lovely lady meant perhaps

Harriet would return to guide me through another adventure that this time might get me killed.

I really should get back to work, not that anybody paid any attention to the reports I wrote. Every day I sit in my broom closet with a stack of major English language newspapers piled high on my desk. Every day I sift through these papers looking for patterns of misbehaviour and glitches in the Universe.

My self-absorption is interrupted by a knock on the door. Whoever it is doesn't wait for my permission to enter, it's Roger, waving his prized writing instrument in the air like a maestro of manipulation that I am positive he thinks he is.

"Hello, dear boy, I see you've settled into your new digs."

He really is a pompous twit, which is standard for the Savile Row types who occupy the Top Floor; I wouldn't care, except for the fact I think he is a treasonous villain.

"I see you found your fabulous pen. It goes nicely with your new designer threads; an upgrade from the tweed and leather patches." I tried my best to be sarcastic. He ignores my tone and acknowledges the pseudo compliment.

"Kind of you to say, old chap, especially under the circumstances. I know we've had our ups and downs, but like all good gentlemen, we manage to accept our fate and move on."

"Sure Roger, I'm happy to move on."

"Spoken like a man not concerned with working for a living." Roger is well aware of my financial wellbeing, the result of an ancient Uncle whose sole pleasure in life was making money.

"In any case, Harry, I have a job for you. Something right up your alley; a visit to a new showing at the Q Gallery. There is an exhibition of figurative abstracts by the wife of the ex-US Attorney General. I believe she is considered quite accomplished, not that I go in for that sort of thing. More of I horse and hound man myself. Be that as it may, here's the invite, be there on time and take in the event."

"And what exactly am I looking for"

"Well, Harry, old chap, you know how it is. We never really know what we are looking for. Just keep your eyes open and report on anything that feels off. Fly-on-the-wall sort of thing. You know what to do, you seem so good at snooping. This

could be your opportunity to erase that unfortunate red ring around your reputation." He doesn't
wait for my response. He drops the invitation on
my desk and leaves. I gather Roger didn't want
the smell of disinfectant left by my predecessor
to get all over his brand new British tailoring.

I was actually looking forward to the assignment.
I open my laptop and the first thing I notice is the
headline, "Anna Marshall Marcel, wife of the ex-
US Attorney General, Displays Her New Work".
The article goes on to explain that her new figurative abstracts were inspired by her unfortunate
recent automobile accident. She describes the
experience as transformative.

My attention is lured from the art news by a
sidebar advertisement for the pitch girl's new
television series, a ripoff of Peter O'Donnell's
goofy comic strip and 1966 movie, *Modesty
Blaise,* starring Monica Vitti and Terence Stamp.
If Harriet shows up, perhaps I can be her Ter-
rence Stamp, a guy could do worse.

Show And Tell

I've recently made some changes in my life. With my career in the dumpster and Harriet gone, I needed something to keep my brain cells active. As you are aware, my only true passion, other than Harriet, is abstract expressionist art.

My mentor in art, tradecraft, and bureaucratic gamesmanship was the late Commander Bowley, who owned the Bowley Gallery, a front that allowed him to travel the world making deals with foreign agents that only occasionally involved oil paint on canvas.

With Bowley gone, I bought the gallery, which included the building on Hazelton Lanes. It's nice to be rich. I know there was some confusion about Bowley's demise the last time we communicated, but that cerebral hiccup has been clarified: the man is most certainly dead.

I converted the top floor of the building into a Bauhaus infused retreat with enough room to display my personal collection along with a large enough studio that allowed me to take out my frustrations by chucking acrylic onto large pieces of stretched canvas. None of it ever amounted to anything but recyclable junk, but the enjoyment is in the effort, despite the inevitable failure and frustration. Why should my creative endeavours be any more successful than my less than Bondian career?

I arrive at the Q Gallery at around nine o'clock with my invitation in hand wearing my best custom tailoring and a cashmere turtleneck for that *I'm arty too* look. Oddly enough, the first person I run into is Mercury, my gallery manager, here to check out the competition. She is surprised to see me; I rarely attend these events and instead rely on her talented eye to cull the weak from the herd. She appears a bit put-out by my presence.

I generally keep my gallery involvement to a minimum, but I do check the books to make sure she's not inflating the expenses. I would be very surprised and disappointed to learn she was taking advantage, but employees will be employees, and despite the friendly smiles, resentment towards bosses is not uncommon.

The fact is, I am extremely fond of Mercury as she is both good at finding what I like and at making money out of an enterprise that is generally a losing proposition. Besides, I have no time to run an art gallery or to deal with the often demanding clientele. Mercury is extraordinarily knowledgeable and professionally gracious but she can be a formidable opponent as I have witnessed on more than one occasion when deals get cocked-up. As anyone who knows these things will tell you, Mercury can be a volatile substance.

We say our hellos, and I assure her that my presence will not interfere with her duties. She knows I work at the consulate in some capacity and is smart enough to not ask questions. Mercury moves on to work the room and snag potential buyers that she might convince to pay our gallery a visit.

I start to make the rounds when I spot a familiar face, it's Harriet. I almost expected her to be here. Even I recognize that her presence seems to coincide with the appearance of the advertising pitch girl who recently reemerged on the scene. Harriet looks at me; her eyes move to a shabby little man with a limp, lingering in the corner. It's as if she's signalling me of the scruffy little man's existence. She takes a step towards me but stops.

I feel the presence of someone behind me. The smell of expensive perfume and cheap champagne assaults my senses. If whoever it is was any closer, we'd have to get a room, "It's about fucking time you showed up." It's the artist, wife of the former US Attorney General.

"The work is excellent. I particularly like this one," as I point to the four by eight canvas in front of me. "It reminds me of Dan McCaw's work." I meant it as a compliment, the work is very good.

"Don't be an ass. Let's get this over so I can sell this stuff. I'll need the dough to survive when the shit hits the fan." She pauses to calm herself, she is struggling to maintain her composure. "And don't think this is just for the money, these people are nuts; they're intent on ruining everything."

Artists do have a reputation for being eccentric but this is very strange. I don't know who she thinks I am or what she thinks is about to happen. Whatever it is, it has obviously pushed her off the rails. She manages to settle herself. "I received the payment this morning. I'll show you the one. It already has a red dot."

I guess this is what Roger meant when he said to keep my eyes open and report anything that was off. It's the report part that concerns me.

If Roger is a Philby-wannabe and Anna Marcel is simply crazy, then it probably doesn't matter, but if Marcel's apparent delusions are somehow real then there may be significant unintended consequences no matter what I do.

It doesn't escape me that this whole thing may be a setup to finally flush me down the drain as retribution for framing Roger for a couple of murders I committed, despite the fact he ended up on the Top Floor and I in the basement.

I had no idea what was happening, but I decided to go with the flow; after all, Harriet is here, and that must mean something or somebody was up to no good.

Marcel interrupts my mental disappearance. "Pay attention for Christ's sake. You should know I had three buyers that wanted that piece. And the Chinese and Russians would pay through the nose to get their hands on the information, but I'm a fucking patriot. You're lucky I'm a goddam decent human-being, not like those fascist fuckers in the White House…"

Her tirade is interrupted by the owner of the Q, "Anna, there is an important buyer, who wants to meet you." She points to the shabby little man in the corner.

"Can't you see I'm busy. I'll be there in a minute, now fuck-off."

Boy is this bitch a charmer. She grabs me by the arm and drags me over to a painting of an abstract man and woman, neither has a definable face. The figures seem to be embracing, perhaps having sex. The painting is thick with pigment and muted tones accented by splashes of vibrant red and gold. Both characters have full-body hexagonal tattoos that wrap around their bodies

"I love it."

"Who gives a shit. All the information you need is there. Make sure it gets to the right people. Where do you want it sent?"

I hand her one of Mercury's business cards. She looks at it, snorts, and walks away. I follow her with my eyes as she approaches the gallery owner and the shabby little man with a limp. She instantly transforms herself into a pleasant hawker of creative sophistication.

Harriet appears out of nowhere, "Quite the lady, your new girlfriend, and I thought we were *a thing.*"

Just then, Mercury approaches me, "I made some interesting contacts; want to meet them?"

"No, I'll leave that to you. I prefer to be a man of mystery." She smiles; she is a very pretty woman.

"Okay boss, man of mystery."

"Oh, by the way, buy Number 9 and have it delivered to the gallery. And they'll also be sending Number 3, the red and gold one."

"Since when..." she stops.

"Don't you like them?"

"Sure they're good."

"So? What's the problem?"

"No problem, You're the boss."

"Don't be upset. This is my business, understand, not our business."

Mercury is a smart girl. "Sure, boss, I get it, consulate business, not our business." She's smiles and squeezes my hand. She wanders off to snag a few more potential buyers.

I turn expecting to see Harriet, but she's gone. No worries, the game has started, and everybody's in play. She'll turn up again, sooner or later.

Tap Dancing With Roger

I arrive at my humble dungeon early the next morning. I admit to being rather unsure of the peculiar events of the previous evening.

Did it all happened as remembered or was it a concocted episode of the ongoing mental movie I'm accused of creating to add excitement to a rather lacklustre career? Or maybe, it was an attempt to conjure the lovely Harriet from the deep recesses of my possibly corrupted brain?

What should I tell Roger, if anything? You understand my dilemma; I believe Roger is a sleeper: a mole recruited in college and placed in a position where he can slowly work his way into a position of authority where he can be of the most benefit to some foreign government looking to do us harm, or maybe just to keep an eye on us. After all, the Cambridge Five does indicate a history of sloppy recruitment and the *Sister* business does point to the Americans as Roger's handlers.

I have to be careful not to cry wolf as I've been previously accused of by Roger and the former higher-ups. They all think I'm a bit mad.

As you know I do have a rich imagination and a highly developed case of Pareidolia that often has me seeing things that aren't there, an issue that often makes me question the very existence of my Harriet. Is she real or just a delusional side-kick invented to guide me through my musings of potential conspiratorial cabals. My thoughts are interrupted by Roger's extravagant writing instrument tapping on the front page of *The New York Times* that sits on my desk in front of me.

"Are you here, dear boy, or have you fled to that place you go to when things get sticky?"

I look up into Roger's vapid facade, "I'm considering what to write in my report."

"Oh no, dear boy, no reports, nothing in writing. Let's keep this little enterprise of ours hush-hush. If what I suspect is happening is real, then the consequences could be significant. We have to hold our cards close to the vest. I don't have to tell you this could be a tricky situation. Neither one of us wants to end up on the wrong side of this business." The more he talked the more I considered not telling him anything.

"Well, I did buy one of Marcel's paintings."

"Is that relevant?"

"Perhaps. But I don't see how."

"I don't understand."

"She approached me as if she knew me. She started to go on about some stuff, but honestly, I thought she was stoned."

"Humm… interesting… as you know she was in a major car accident the day after Bigelow committed suicide. The previous evening's event was supposed to be a birthday party, but instead, it became a fractious shambles."

"Any idea what the source of the problem was?"

"You know how these things are; put a bunch of A-type personalities together in a room, all with an agenda, add a whole lot of booze, and you're sure to create some fireworks. Word is, some senior Cabinet members aren't happy with the new direction the White House is taking. It has the distinct smell of that unfortunate 1933 Wall Street business. And there seems to be an unusual number of unlucky accidents that have allowed the President to make some dramatic changes in his staff, men with a lot of stars on their shoulders. If you catch my drift?"

Roger rubs his chin to show he is thinking hard. "You have no idea, who she thought you were?"

"No sir, not a clue."

"Perhaps that car accident knocked a screw loose. That bump on the head might have induced some kind of facial delusion like Fregoli. Is Marcel still in town?"

"You know she's a Canadian, born and raised in Toronto. She met her husband when she went to Yale on an art scholarship. I believe she still owns her parents' place in Woodbridge. From what I read she comes up here to get away from Washington where she can paint without interruption or official obligations."

"Why don't you get in touch with the owner of the Q Gallery to arrange a visit. Tell her, you want to discuss a commission for some big-shot."

I was playing a dangerous game by not telling Roger about the second painting. If Roger was a mole, telling him could create a problem; on the other hand, if he was just a pompous prick, fond of playing Machiavellian games, then I was surely looking for trouble by not telling him everything.

Whatever is going on revolved around the painting Marcel assumed I bought and who she thinks I am. Whoever did buy that painting would be pissed when they find out she gave it to the wrong guy. Visiting Marcel may place me right in the centre of someone's crosshairs.

Maybe Roger knows me better than I know myself? Maybe he was setting me up as the mole to cover his tracks? I couldn't help but feel I was screwed no matter what I did. If Harriet was here, she'd know what to do.

A Puzzle In Pigment

After Roger left I called Margret Kennedy, owner of the Q Gallery. I told her I owned the Bowley and that I had a client who is interested in commissioning Marcel to do a large mural for the lobby of one of his office towers. Of course, she would receive her usual commission. It was all bullshit but some kind of ruse was needed to get me through the front door.

She informed me that Anna had some sort of episode after the opening. Perhaps an after-the-fact letdown brought on by the stress of preparing for the big event. She went on to describe how she drove the temperamental artist to the airport to catch the redeye to Washington once she settled down.

At that point, I stopped listening. She continued to push for an alternative arrangement for the non-existent commission but I put her off with some lame excuse. From my brief experience with Marcel, it seems she is overdue for some sorely-needed intensive therapy, but I suppose I should be the last one to judge.

Whether her anxiety was due to the stress of the opening, her car accident, or something else, one thing was sure; the woman was in trouble. She acted very strangely at the art gallery.

Whatever was going on, it seemed the large red and gold figurative abstract was the key to the puzzle. It did not escape me that the recent seemingly bizarre events could be one of my own highly developed fantasies. Roger calls them delusions. They could also be part of Roger's continuing plot to label me a looney-bird and unfit for duty. Getting rid of the only person in the shop that thought he was a double would be the right move for a Philby clone. Or Roger could be right and I was off my rocker.

My mind went back to the painting. I wonder if it will actually be sent to me, or maybe Kennedy caught the error and redirected it to the right buyer. I called Mercury to see if either or both of the paintings arrived.

"Hello, Bowley Gallery, Mercury Collins speaking."

"It's me. Did those two paintings from last night arrive?"

"Yes, they came about an hour ago. Along with a gift from the artist."

"A gift? What kind of gift?"

"A bottle of Hine Antique Cognac with a note."

"What's it say?"

"It's just one word... *Evidence.*"

"*Evidence?* You sure?"

"Harry, I can read. I did go to school."

"Have the red and gold painting hung in my apartment and the other in the gallery."

"You want me to sell the gallery piece?"

"Yes... but put it up for sale with a ridiculously inflated price. If you get a buyer, take down all the contact information and tell them it's from my personal collection and you have to check with me before you can sell it. If they ask if I have any more of her work, tell them no."

There's a long pause at the other end of the line. "Do you understand my instructions?"

"Yes of course. This is *your* business, not *our* business."

"Smart girl. One day you'll make a formidable Igor to some mad Frankenstein."

"I believe I already am, but much prettier and with better posture."

I laugh, "That is most certainly true. And take a long hard look at the red and gold one. There is something there beyond pigment and canvas, but I don't know what."

"What do you want me to do with the Cognac?"

"Put it on the island in my kitchen."

"Be careful, Harry, I like having you around." We hang up.

I arrive back at the gallery around eight o'clock. Mercury is sitting in her office eating a salad.

"I thought you'd be gone by now."

"I've been waiting for you."

I sit down across from her desk. I'm tired and my brain hurts from trying to figure out what was going on and how much trouble I was in. The last thing I wanted to do was get Mercury involved in this mess.

"About those Marcel paintings…"

'Something happen?"

"After we got the gallery Marcel hung I had Billy take the red and gold one up to your apartment. While I was inspecting the gallery painting to make sure it wasn't damaged in transit a strange little man with a bad suit and a noticeable limp came in demanding I give him the painting."

"You mean he wanted to buy it."

"No! He said the painting was his. He tried to take it off the wall but I stopped him."

"You stopped him? How?"

"I kicked him in his bad leg."

I couldn't help but laugh. She laughed too, as I said before, you don't mess with Mercury. "Then what happened?"

"Oh… exactly what you'd expect. He yelped like a little girl and started swearing. Once he ran out of curses he started to threaten me, but Billy came down from your place waving a hammer, so the little weasel skulked out muttering something about dire consequences." She pauses to consider what she just told me as if it hadn't dawned on her before. "It seems *your* business and *our* business is getting rather commingled."

She noticed the concerned look on my face. "Not to worry, I can handle myself. And besides Billy is always in the back with his hammer."

If you hadn't already guessed, Billy is our framer and Mercury's assistant. I wasn't comfortable with the idea of Mercury and Billy being involved in whatever was going on.

"I took a close look at your red and gold piece like you asked and I think your mystery is hiding in plain sight."

"Why? What did you find?"

"I gather you didn't take much chemistry at that fancy private school you went to."

"Actually, private schools are called public schools in Britain. So technically I went to a fancy public school."

"Well, that explains a lot about the British."

"I should be offended, but remember, I'm only half British, so I'm only half offended."

"Do you want to know what I found or would you prefer to verbally joust with me a bit."

"I would gladly joust with you anytime, but let's get to it as I'm tired and I'm sure you want to go home."

"I do worry about you, Harry. I don't know what you do at the consulate, but I know Commander Bowley was your friend and mentor, so I can only assume you run in the same circles. I'm very fond of you, so do me a favour won't you?"

"Of course, anything."

"Please don't get killed."

"I'll do my best. Perhaps the painting might help keep me vertical."

"Ah yes, the painting. Well, if you took chemistry as a lad back in the old country, you'd have recognized those hex tattoos as chemical formulae. Each figure has a different formula."

I'm stunned. "Shit… is it really that simple?"

"Not exactly. The hexes are wrapped around the bodies so it's hard to tell if you have all the information and of course the elements are missing or hidden somehow. I'm afraid that's the best I can do, perhaps you can contact someone at the university who might be able to figure it out."

I get up and kiss Mercury on the cheek. You're the best. Now go home and get some rest."

She smiles, "It was fun, I like puzzles. And you... be careful, there is definitely something fishy about this whole business."

Oil Paint and Cognac

Mercury locked-up the gallery while I went up-stairs to relax and try and figure out what other secrets were hidden in the Marcel. Billy stayed late to finish some framing.

I put a frozen pizza in the microwave and open the Hine's. I pour an overdose of the cognac into a Bormioli Crescendo brandy snifter. I know, cognac and frozen pizza aren't exactly a five-star combination but then what's the point of being rich if you can't do stupid shit like eating three-dollar pizza with two-hundred-dollar cognac.

I turn on the television and search for the news. What I get is a commercial; the all-news station seems to be profitably divided into equal parts of breathless breaking news reports and advertisements for prescription drugs that seem to do more damage to the human body than anything a hypochondriac paranoid could imagine. I'm only half surprised when the commercial is for the new cable television series starring everybody's favourite advertising it-girl.

I go into the bedroom to change into jeans, a black cotton turtle neck, and a matching un-tucked flannel over-shirt. I retrieve my pizza and cognac and head for the couch that is occupied by my favourite femme fatale, Harriet.

"Hello Harry, long time, no see."

I take a drink from the snifter and bite into my pizza. I plop myself down beside her on the couch. She touches my leg, sending shivers through my body.

"It's nice to see you too, my love."

"How did you get…"

"…in?" She finishes my sentence with a laugh. "Come now Harry, we've been through this before, haven't we? Besides, your Billy is a sweet lad and that Mercury, my goodness, she is a dish. I should be jealous, in fact, I am… a little. But be honest my love, you only have eyes for me."

I take another bite of pizza.

"Not talking to me? Angry at my absence? I am sorry Harry, my dear, but I have had things to do: double-crossers to foil, villains to defeat, and plots to uncover."

"Really?"

"Oh be kind Harry, forgive a girl for her trespass-es, after all, we are *a thing,* aren't we?"

I sigh in exasperation. She knows she had me wrapped around her finger and could push me in any direction she wanted.

"Okay Harriet I give up, you win."

"That's better, my sweet. Friends again as we should be and will always be."

"So who do you work for this time?"

"The good guys, Harry, always the good guys."

"And exactly who are the bad guys?"

"You know how these things work, Harry. All will be revealed in good time."

"Know anything about a creepy little man with a limp?" She ignores the question pretending to be distracted with the red and gold painting.

"How about Roger? Is Roger on your list?"

She looks me in the eye with her piercing green disks. My knees buckle despite the fact I'm sit-ting. "That remains to be seen, my love, but enough about that sorry situation. Let's talk about this painting you've managed to get your hands on. I won't ask how you did it, but my goodness, how you've grown. You really are a big-boy spy now, aren't you, my love?"

"Do you know who paid for it?"

"What makes you think it wasn't me?"

"You, why?

"Information, dear Harry, information. It's the key to solving the riddle, the missing piece of the puzzle, the knot that unwraps the enigma." She laughs at her Churchillian string of cliches. And so we sit and stare at the painting for what seems a very long time.

Finally, Harriet speaks, "Infrared Reflectography, that will give us the answer to what's behind the hexagonal mystery."

I stand to shake the cobwebs from my brain. I get up close to the canvas as if proximity would reveal its secrets. It doesn't. I collapse into a leather Walter Gropius armchair that is more art than chair. I'm exhausted from my verbal affair with the lovely Harriet.

Infrared Reflectography, why didn't I think of that, but of course, if Harriet is just a figment of my imagination, a loose electrical impulse misfiring in my noggin, then, I did think of it.

Yes I know, you're probably sick of this whole, is she real or not bullshit, but as I've told you before, this is my movie so fuck you. Besides, anybody who knows anything about cinema knows it's unrequited love that keeps the paying public in their seats. Close the deal and your franchise is *kaput*. So there it is, it's my story, deal with it.

I feel very strange as if I'm falling from a great height. I grab the arm of the Gropius to stop my descent. I wake with a start. I must have fallen asleep. Harriet is gone. The sun is shining down through the skylight, it's morning.

Fuck, what the hell happened? I've had the most bizarre dream, more hallucination than dream. It was so real, so vivid, yet I have no recollection of any of it. I turn on the television and switch to the all-news channel, just to make sure I don't miss any *breaking news*. I apologize for the sarcasm, but really, not everything is important, and not everything is equal. Some stuff is just more important than other stuff, and that stuff should be treated as such.

I feel sick. I make my way to the bathroom. My head is splitting and my stomach is rumbling. Maybe pizza and cognac aren't a good dinner combination after-all.

The reflection in the mirror is a pasty shade of titanium white mixed with sap green. I'm about to heave. I manage to empty my guts into the Kohler completely obliterating my fancy custom crapper in vomit. What the hell just happened. I feel like I've been drugged.

Harriet… no, I don't believe it. She wouldn't, would she?"

Three-hundred-and-fifty miles away Anna Marcel walks into a fancy Georgetown coffee shop and orders a double Espresso Macchiato. The place is busy with the morning rush of caffeine addicts.

A pair of shabby hooligans in torn hoodies and mud-splattered ripped jeans barge into the coffee shop. They wave semi-automatic Glock 19s in the air demanding whatever money is in the cash register.

While one of the thugs fills his pockets with the bills handed-over by the petrified barista, the other spots Marcel's three-carat diamond ring. He demands she turn it over.

Her response is in keeping with her rather prickly personality. "Fuck-off and die!" He shoots her in the head. What nobody notices is the two presumed street thugs are wearing eight-hundred dollar black Fendi sneakers.

Back in Toronto, the familiar breaking news theme announces something important just broke. The anchor interrupts the tirade being inflicted on the audience by some White House lackey complaining about the news medias coverage of the President's recent appointments.

"Well-known artist and wife of former Attorney General, Anna Marcel has been killed…"

"Oh god… I have to puke again."

Command and Control

A black stretch-Lincoln Town Car with bullet-proof windows sits in the K Street parking garage of the Washington Harbour mall. The two men in the front wear dark custom suits that give the distinct impression they should have been made with epaulettes and brass buttons. If people were more observant they would notice the sartorial *faux pax* in the form of black Fendi sneakers on their feet. The expensive casual footwear does provide for a quick first step if one is needed; far more useful for two bodyguards than a pair of heavy-soled brogues.

Malcolm Blackburn, CEO of Blackburn Security sits in the back reading reports. Blackburn Security is a military contractor specializing in supplemental services for off-book operations. In other words, it's a private army contracted to provide services that the various Congressional over-site committees would find questionable, if not downright objectionable.

A nondescript silver Chevy pulls up alongside the limousine. A rumpled little man with a limp gets out and enters the back seat of the Lincoln.

Blackburn doesn't bother to even look up from the report he is reading. "So did you get the painting or did you fuck that up too."

"Listen, Malcolm, I'm a goddam scientist, not a field agent."

"You... are whatever the fuck I tell you to be."

"Don't get on your high horse with me, Malcolm. This operation doesn't work without me. I'm part of the command structure just like you. We can't depend on your band of mercenaries to control everybody; we need the drugs if we ever want to make this work. There's no way we can do it with marshal law alone. There are just too many guns out there. We need the military and the drugs to keep the yahoos in line. You need me, so have some respect."

"Calm down. Don't get so excited or you'll pop a blood vessel and will have to give you some of your own medicine."

"You can't get rid of me as easily as you did the others. You're getting sloppy, Malcolm, that Marcel business was bad. What if your thugs were caught on camera."

The two men in the front turn around and give the little man with a limp a hard look.

"Don't worry about my guys, they're professionals. You just get that fucking painting. We paid for it, why did they deliver it to someone else?"

"When Marcel left the camp, the drugs were still in her system, that's probably why she crashed. When her head hit the windshield, she suffered a brain trauma. She seemed okay after the accident, but she must have had some form of DMS."

"What the hell is DMS?"

"Delusional Misidentification Syndrome, a kind of Fregoli Delusion. Patients with Fregoli believe different people are the same person in disguise. She must have thought that the guy at the art gallery was me."

"Why? Does he wear bad suits and walk with a limp?"

"You really are an asshole, Malcolm. No, he doesn't look like me. I just explained to you, the woman had a brain injury. You mess with these drugs and you're going to have unintended consequences."

"I see. She thought a handsome six-foot Englishman was a five-foot-three weasel with a limp."

"Prick!"

One of the men in the front seat turns around, "Colonel, you want us to retrieve the merchandise?"

The little man with the limp objects, "You can't just go around killing people."

"Sure we can. What the hell do you think we've been doing, and that my little friend, includes using your designer drugs. You can't make Filet Mignon without killing a few cows."

The two men in the front seat wait for their instructions, "You two go to Toronto and get in touch with *Hicks,* but not at his office. Tell him he either gets that painting or you'll do it. He'll get the message."

The little man with the limp is relieved he doesn't have to retrieve the artwork. His leg still hurts where the woman kicked him. "Great, try not to have your boys make a mess like they did with Marcel."

"You're so worried about them killing someone, you go with them."

The little man thinks for a second, "What about the Secretary of Health and the Surgeon General. There's no way we can get enough drugs into the population without their help."

"Don't worry about them. The President is going to announce another cabinet shuffle. Our people will be put in place."

Break-In At The Bowley

I'm tired: tired of the Machiavellian games everyone is playing; tired of wanting Harriet so des-
perately, and tired of my addiction to failure and
frustration. I'm tired of the whole silly mess. Why
couldn't they just leave me alone in my smelly
basement closet with my newspapers?

I'm a simple man, satisfied with a solitary existence and an overripe imagination. Reality, fantasy, delusion, it's all the same to me, all elements
of the script that plays in my head on an endless
ever-changing loop.

I stretch out on top of the bed. There is no point
in trying to sleep, my mind is far too busy editing
the events of the past few days. I decide to watch
some television. maybe it will distract me for a
while. It's Saturday, almost midnight, I put on the
channel that always plays Film Noir classics.

The screen comes alive with Bogie and Greenstreet doing their thing in *The Maltese Falcon*. I
love the genre despite the realization that many
of the lesser examples are just cheaply made
filler, but when they get it right, like the story of
the *black bird*, then my god it's wonderful.

To hear the crisp verbal duelling between Bogie and Greenstreet is to listen to dialogue the way it's supposed to be written and delivered. Nobody writes like that anymore, except maybe Tarantino, and maybe Sorkin....

Gutman

"I distrust a man who says when. He's got to be careful not to drink too much... because he's not to be trusted when he does. Well, sir... here's to plain speaking and clear understanding."

Thank you, Sidney, "plain speaking and clear understanding" is exactly what I need. The movie goes to commercial and you know what the ad is for: the pitch girl's new *Modesty Blaise* remake.

I feel a presence hovering over me. I'd fallen asleep; it was all a dream, Harriet is trying to wake me, "Harry, there's someone downstairs."

"How did you..."

"Not now, Harry, someone is stealing the Marcel." That cleared the cobwebs fast. I managed to get myself upright.

"Harry, take the Beretta."

I reach into the bedside table drawer and remove the APX sub-compact. The red and gold Marcel still hangs in my living room.

I open the balcony door and step out onto the landing that overhangs the gallery. Two men in dark suits and black sneakers are taking the gallery Marcel off the wall. They are being direct- ed by a shabbily dressed little man who appears to have a pronounced limp. I take three steps down the balcony staircase.

"You have two seconds to put that painting back on the wall before I paint that empty space with your brain matter."

One of the suits goes for his gun. I fire, hitting him in the shoulder. I was aiming for his chest. The impact spins him around as he tries to re- turn fire. His shot hits the space between two very large, very expensive abstracts. It's dark in the gallery but I see the other suit is considering his chances.

"I wouldn't if I was you. My aim gets better the more awake I become."

The little man with the limp looks at me and then at the man with the suit still standing. His pal is bleeding all over my gallery floor. "Get him out of here and get Hicks."

"Bringing in fresh reinforcements are we?"

The little man barks his instructions again, "Get the fuck out of here and get Hicks."

The uninjured suit takes his pal and they leave. The little man with a limp just stands and waits. A few minutes later the gallery door opens and Roger steps in. "Good evening Harry, or should I say good morning?"

"You… just what the hell do you think you're doing, Roger? Take your little friend and get the fuck out of my place before I shoot the whole bunch of you."

"Calm yourself, dear boy, it's late and none of us have had our beauty sleep, so let's all just relax and work this out like gentlemen."

"I was right all along. Your name was on the list. I ought to shoot you where you stand. The Queen will give me a fucking metal."

"Oh, Harry, you and your list. Forget the goddam list for a minute. That's old business and look at how that worked out. Me on the Top Floor, and you in a basement broom closet."

"Maybe a bullet to your head would put things right?"

"Afraid not, dear boy. There are more black suits and little men with limps than you can shake a stick at. Let's talk this over, Harry, no point in you getting your knickers in a twist over this. You already have a reputation. You wouldn't want to blot your copybook any further, now, would you? It's time for us to put the past where it belongs and get on the same side of things."

I make my way to the third stair from the bottom providing me with enough safe distance to talk and still get off a clean kill shot. Roger comes closer, so the little man can't hear us. He drops the *dear boy* bullshit and gets straight to the point, "Listen to me carefully, Harry, don't be an ass." I'm surprised by his *plain speaking and clear understanding*, "It's the gimp's painting. He paid for it. Besides, *it's not the droids he's looking for, is it?"*

I had to smile, Roger, seemed to be full of surprises. "Okay, Roger, take the painting, but I expect a full explanation, first thing Monday."

"Of course, dear boy, a full and complete explanation, at least, as far as I can take you."

The little man with the limp, the one Roger, called the gimp, was getting impatient. "Is he giving us the fucking painting or do I have to have my men come back." I ignore the little man and his apparent frustration.

Roger looks me in the eye, "So can we take the painting without any further trouble?"

I nod. Roger turns to signal the little man that a truce has been signed, but I grab his shoulder, "A full explanation, agreed?"

"Agreed."

"One more thing. Why did he call you Hicks?"

Roger smiles, "Harry, you're a very nice young man, very imaginative, quite good at your job, but sometimes you are extremely transparent. I know how you think. I know what you think I am, but things are not always what they seem. Hicks is a bit of a joke. The Americans do have a peculiar sense of humour. Think Cambridge Five: Maclean, Burgess, Cairncross, Blunt, and your favourite, Philby. Naturally, they didn't get it quite right, I believe Philby was code name, Sonny and

Burgess was code name, Hicks." He turns and together with the little man they take the wrong Marcel from my gallery.

Why did Harriet imply she bought the painting? What did I expect; the breadcrumbs she left for clues were always full of false steps and misdirections. Perhaps it's my brain turning things over making a stew out of random facts, but enough for one evening. I lock the front door behind them and go back upstairs to my apartment.

Harriet isn't there.

Clean Up and Move On

There is nothing like an armed robbery perpetrated by your boss to keep you from having a good night's sleep. My mind is racing with random thoughts and flashes of near insight that seems to be just out of reach. I open my laptop and stare at the screen. I think things are starting to take shape although their form is more amorphous than concrete, but then, I am good at visualizing things, even when nothing is there. Who says being nuts doesn't have its advantages.

What is it that Roger said that day in my office, *"Word is, some senior Cabinet members aren't happy with the new direction the White House is taking. It has the distinct smell of that unfortunate 1933 Wall Street business. And there seems to be an unusual number of unfortunate accidents ... If you catch my drift?"*

At the time, I didn't pay too much attention to what he was saying. I was more concerned with my own sorry descent into the basement corridors of power. When Roger mentioned 1933 and Wall Street, I instantly thought of the Depression, but now that I think about it, he was trying to tell me something by linking it to the series of accidents, injuries, and deaths that have befallen senior Cabinet and White House Advisors.

It didn't take long for me to find the reference, "The Wall Street Putsch of 1933". Various Wall Street financiers and business leaders tried to overthrow the government. It seemed fascism was more acceptable than Roosevelt's progressive New Deal. If it wasn't for a whistleblower, Retired Marine Corps Major General Smedley Butler, America could be a very different kind of country... maybe Roger's cryptic message is a warning that it could happen again.

Roger knew about the red and gold Marcel in my apartment and he still went along with the little man with a limp's mistaken notion that the gallery Marcel was the prize, the black bird of our little late-night playdate.

Before I shot Freddy, my mechanic in the head, he told me the whole *Sister Project* business was an American plot to fuck with the Canadian election and not a Russian one. Did Roger's name on that list mean he was working for the Americans or was he working for our Vauxhall Cross masters keeping an eye on the American Benedict Arnolds? After last night's little talk it certainly seemed to be a possibility, either that or Roger was playing me like a Stradivarius.

The whole thing is as clear as dishwater. Where the hell is Harriet when I need her? I decided to let the information percolate for a while. I still had the painting and that suspicious bottle of Hine's that made me sick. Originally I thought the ambiguous note with the single word "Evidence" only referred to the painting, and the cognac was a peace-offering for Marcel's rather rude behaviour, but now I'm not so sure. Maybe the booze is evidence as well.

I notice there's a message on my phone. It's Roger, "About our little *tête-à-tête*, I'm afraid it will have to be postponed, I'm off to Washington for some meetings. Don't be alarmed, old boy, we'll have our chat. In the meantime, you might want to contact Professor Krish Bakshi an expert in Infrared Reflectography at the Art Gallery of Ontario and Dr. Arnold Klein in the Department of Chemistry at York." Roger seemed to know a lot more about what I was doing than I did.

I manage to get in touch with both Professor Bakshi and Dr. Klein despite the fact it's Sunday. They initially aren't pleased to be interrupted on their days off, but when I mention it's a matter of national security and that I work for Professor Roger Ames, their attitude becomes almost solicitous.

After I finish my calls, coffee, and egg white omelette, I make my way downstairs to see what kind of shape the gallery is in after last night's unscheduled event. As I come down the stairs I see Mercury mopping the blood from the gallery floor and Billy puttying the bullet hole in the wall. No-one says a word about the missing painting. Mercury looks at me with her beautiful blue eyes. "Have a nice evening?"

I ignore the sarcasm. "Have Billy wrap-up the red and gold Marcel and have it sent over to a Professor Krish Bakshi at the Art Gallery of Ontario."

After some further discussion of gallery housekeeping issues, I went upstairs took a shower and put on fresh clothes. I put the bottle of Hine's in a plastic bag and head out the back to my vintage 1954 MG. Next stop, York University, to pay a visit to Dr. Arnold Klein.

When I get to my car I notice someone is sitting in the passenger seat. I get in. The passenger turns in her seat, leans over the gearshift, and kisses me on the cheek, "Good morning, Harry." I put the car in gear and head for Dr. Klein's lab with Harriet at my side.

I Never Did Like Beer

Harriet sits quietly in the passenger seat of my MG while we drive. I am content just to have her at my side. Finally, she speaks, "I'm happy to see you as well, Harry."

"I didn't say anything."

"You don't have to, my love... two peas in a pod, remember."

"Oh yes, I remember."

"Have you connected all the dots.?"

"No. I haven't. I've got a painting, a bottle of booze, and a headache. None of it adds up. And Roger is playing Cups and Balls with competing interests under every cup."

"And whose balls do you think are in play?"

I couldn't help but smile despite myself, "You don't think this is serious?"

"Yes, of course, I do. The question is, whose interests, is Roger promoting?"

"It looks like the Americans, but maybe he's working counterintelligence, who the hell knows?"

Harriet thinks for a minute, "Maybe… it's someone else, a third party with skin in the game."

"Spill it, Harriet. I know you know something, what's the missing piece of the puzzle?"

"We know there's a plot: senior White House advisors and Cabinet Secretaries are being replaced like dead Duracells. Their replacements all seem to have a fondness for epaulettes and gold stars; and Malcolm Blackburn is increasingly more influential, not to mention richer."

"Blackburn's a tool, a means to an end, not an end in itself."

Harriet turns, there's a twinkle in her beautiful green eyes, "What is the secret behind our little black bird of a painting? When in doubt, follow the money. Malcolm Blackburn is rich, but his wife and her sister, the Vice President's wife, are the Mansa Musa of beer."

"The politically tapped-in sisters' Daddy is Winston Pijiu. He's been on everyone's radar ever since his regional brewery exploded onto the national and international scene."

"So where does a small Western regional brewery get the dough to expand to international prominence overnight?"

"I'll bet dollars to yuan if we follow the money it will lead back to Beijing and the Ministry of State Security. The Pijiu sisters are the third ball in our crooked game of Cups."

"That's right Harry my love, the *Sister Project* lives and the Pijiu sisters are the conduit to the real villains in our movie, the Chinese."

We drive the rest of the way to York University in silence. The *Sister Project* is alive and well with new ingredients and a secret sauce of bad mojo. Last year's Canadian interference was merely a preliminary round, now it's the main event with the heavyweights on the card. But where does Roger fit into the picture? Whose side is that pompous ass on? I feel the murky gumbo of forces closing in and I'm stuck in the soup with no way out.

We arrive at York and park. The University was designed by someone who must have thought Toronto is located in Southern California. The parking lot is huge with students forced to park a good twenty minutes from anywhere they want to go, making for rather unpleasant mid-winter walks. Thank goodness it's Spring.

As expected, Harriet insisted on waiting in the car to protect it from student radicals intent on overthrowing the New World Order while damaging my vintage MG along with it. I knew she'd be gone when I returned.

Eventually, with no help from anyone employed at the institution of higher learning, I found Dr. Klein's office and presented him with the bottle of Hine Antique XO Premier Cru Cognac.

I told him of my unfortunate pizza and cognac dinner and the resulting explosion of semi-digested pathogens. I also supplied him with an emailed image of the two faceless Marcel figures covered in hexagonal tattoos that seemed to be formulae of some kind.

He promises to test for any toxins or unnatural substances present in the booze. I tell him to keep the investigation on the q.t. as it's a matter of national security. His chest expands showing exactly how proud of himself he is for being entrusted with such an important state secret.

The Fendi Break-in

Two men wearing overalls and eight-hundred dollar black Fendi running shoes arrive at the Art Gallery of Ontario. A security guard stops them.

"Can I help you?"

The taller of the Fendi men answers, "We're picking up a painting that Professor Bakshi analyzed for the Bowley Gallery." He hands the security guard the clipboard he's holding. The minimum wage security guard looks at the official-looking document with AGTS - Art Gallery Transport Service printed across the top of the page.

"Okay, go ahead. Professor Bakshi's lab is on the lower level, you can't miss it."

The two men arrive at Bakshi's lab and enter without knocking. Bakshi has the Marcel on a large easel. "Can I help you?"

"We're here to pick up the Marcel and return it to the Bowley."

Bakshi looks the two men over. He's skeptical. The smaller man has one arm that hangs loosely from his shoulder as if it has limited mobility.

Bakshi thinks it odd that a man with an obvious injury would be sent on a delivery.

The taller man hands Bakshi the clipboard. He looks down at the paperwork and notices the shoes, the same expensive Fendi sneakers his wife bought him for his birthday.

"Listen, fellows, I haven't analyzed the artwork yet. I'll call Mercury and tell her I still need it."

"That's not necessary, Professor. The Bowley needs it back now. I guess they have a hot buyer."

When Billy dropped off the painting, he warned Bakshi that there were dangerous people interested in the secrets the artwork held and under no circumstances should he hand over the painting to anyone but Harry or himself. "It will only take a second, no point, in taking it back and forth more than necessary."

Bakshi turns but before he could get to his desk, the taller Fendi man grabs his shoulder and wheels him around. The Professor tries to strike the fake deliveryman but his attempt is blocked. That's the last thing Professor Krish Bakshi remembers before waking up in an emergency ward at the Mount Sinai Hospital.

With the tainted Cognac in the good chemist's hands, I head for the Consulate. My phone buzzes; I answer; it's Mercury, "Harry, I just got a call from the hospital; Professor Bakshi was injured in a robbery."

"A robbery? You mean they got the Marcel."

"They wouldn't tell me. Bakshi insisted they call you. He wants to see you as soon as possible."

"Which hospital is he in?"

"The Mount Sinai."

I hit the accelerator and head for University Avenue and the Mount Sinai Hospital. I push my little British sports car for all she's worth. Mercury can hear the stream of horns that follow my reckless progress, "Be careful Harry. I rather not have to visit you in the hospital." We hang up.

The traffic in Toronto ranges from horrendous to criminal no matter the time of day or night, but with some judicious backstreet maneuvers, I manage to get to the hospital in fifteen minutes.

It takes me a while to find a parking space. Luckily a family the size of a college football team decides they've inflicted their presence on their poor sick relative enough and decide to go home.

I pull into the vacated spot before someone else grabs it. Parking in downtown Toronto is every man for himself. I find Bakshi in one of those depressing curtained-off cubicles. He appears pale and his head is bandaged.

He looks up at me with a pained expression on his face, "Are you, Harry?"

I show him my Consulate ID which says I'm a Commercial Attaché. He smiles at the obvious and none too subtle official obfuscation.

"I'm sorry, they got the painting. There were two of them and I couldn't..."

"Take it easy, Professor. There's nothing you could have done. Do you remember anything about them?"

"As soon as I saw the two deliverymen were wearing eight-hundred dollar sneakers I knew they were trouble. I told them I hadn't analyzed the painting yet and that I had to call Mercury." He pauses to catch his breath. "That's the last thing I remember before waking up here."

"Too bad you didn't have time to reveal the secrets it's hiding."

"Aah, but I did. I told them I hadn't analyzed it but I just finished when they showed up. Get my phone" He points to his jacket on a metal chair in the corner.

I retrieve his phone and hand it to him. He scrolls through some images. When he finds what he's looking for he hands me the device. "There, that's what's hidden under the pigment."

I look at the image on the phone. It's a map of the United States divided into districts. Blue solid lines emanate from a southern Wyoming location near the Colorado border to each of the areas marked with a blue "D", while red dotted lines find their home in areas marked with a red "R".

"I did notice something else that may be of interest, but my experience with chemistry is more recreational than scientific."

"Tell me."

"Those tattoos on the two faceless figures are definitely chemical formulae. I'm pretty sure one of them is LSD... in school, we used to call it *Lucy In The Sky*, you know, from the Beatles. I can't tell you what the other one is, but it's something, I'm sure of it."

"Great work Professor. You understand you can't tell anyone what you found, nobody, not your wife, girlfriend, or tennis pals. You already got a bump on the head, you don't want anything more dramatic to happen to you."

"Understood, Harry, I'm not looking to be a hero."

"Good. And if somebody from the Consulate comes around, a smug asshole named Roger Ames or Hicks, tell him you found nothing. The delivery guys got the painting before you had a chance to look it over. And whatever you do, don't mention the shoes. Email me those images then delete them from your phone."

"Harry, you're *kinda* scaring me."

"Sorry Professor, but that's exactly what I'm try-ing to do. Just forget this whole thing happened. You fell and hit your head, end of story."

Lucy and The Devil's Breath

I head back to my office to see if I can make any sense out of what I've found out. I have a map of the United States overlaid with some kind of network and two chemical formulae, one of which is probably LSD.

I search Google for district and distribution maps of the USA. It doesn't take long to figure out the districts in the Marcel painting are congressional districts. The "D" and "R" represent areas that are either Democratic or Republican. The colours confused me at first; in Canada, party colours are opposite their closest American counterparts.

The network overlay took me a while longer to decipher. I searched for major corporate backers of both parties. After three cups of coffee and a sumatriptan tablet, I found what I was looking for, Pijiu Brewery's distributor network.

Winston Pijiu, (aka Pijiu Wei), Chairman and CEO of Pijiu Brewery LLC, is known to be a big supporter of the current unhinged American President and a backer of the de facto head of the US government, Vice President Leonard Bowater, husband of Barbara Pijiu Bowater, elder daughter of the beer magnate himself. If that wasn't curious enough, Winston's baby girl is the wife of mercenary magnate Malcolm Blackburn.

Following the digital breadcrumbs is tedious, time-consuming, and not especially legal, but the resources are there to be used as long as you don't get caught; screwup and the price I'll pay for altruistic inquisitiveness, not to mention doing my job, is a reservation in a six by nine concrete bunker in HM Prison Belmarsh.

My somewhat illegal rummaging through a series of Five Eye documents, work product far above my pay grade, made for very interesting reading. The CIA, CSIS, ASIS, NZSIS, and my own MI6 have all designated Pijiu Wei, a senior asset of the Enterprise Division of China's Ministry of State Security, the MSS section responsible for the operation and management of MSS owned front companies and institutions. These false fronts are tasked with *Astroturfing* foreign communities to promote chaos and discontent within the centres of Capitalist competition.

Roger's cryptic warning of a *coup d'état* is starting to come into focus. Everything that's happened recently, including the rumoured bizarre booze and drug-fuelled squabble at Camp David, followed by an unusual rash of senior White House and Cabinet deaths, the appointment of senior military men to replace them, and Anna Marcel's red and gold puzzle in pigment, all add up to a takeover of the US government by private interests sponsored and funded by the People's Republic of China.

The playbook for such attempts historically relies on chaos; create a domestic crisis as the excuse to send in the Blackshirts and declare martial law. The map is my black bird, the key that will ultimately reveal the secret plan.

The phone rings. It's Dr. Klein. "Harry, it's Arnold. I've tested the cognac. I don't think you're going to like what I found."

"Don't tell me, the cognac is laced with LSD."

"Good guess, but it's worse than that. I found Lysergic acid diethylamide and Hyoscine. It's a cocktail of LSD, scopolamine, and booze. This is some dangerous shit. I'm surprised you haven't suffered any after-effects, hallucinations, or strange flashbacks."

"I'm not much of a drinker, Doc, so I guess I only drank enough to make me sick to my stomach."

"You're lucky. By the way, the image of the painting you sent me, confirms it, those hexagonal tattoos are the formulae for LSD and Hyoscine. Someone was desperate to tell you something and someone else was even more determined to stop you from finding it out."

"Thanks, Doc, you've been a great help."

"Is there anything else I can do?"

"Package up the alcohol and your results and send them to The Bowley Gallery, Attention Mercury Collins. Delete everything you've done from any servers, hard drives, or computers. And shred any paper trail. This stuff never existed."

"Sure Harry, I get it…" He pauses as if he has something else to say.

"Is there something else you want to tell me?"

"Well, this whole thing has got me thinking, but I hesitate to bring it up. I don't want you to think I'm one of those conspiracy nutcases."

"Doc, you know the old saying, 'if it walks like a duck and quacks like a duck, it's probably…"

Klein cuts in, "*Lucy's Breath.*"

"What's *Lucy's Breath?*"

"There's scuttlebutt floating around certain circles, but nothing anybody can confirm. You know how these things are, Harry, things never really go away, they just morph into something worse."

"Come on Doc, let's have it."

"Arno Koch, he's a crazy son-of-a-bitch, but a genius. He was a young East German chemist that worked for the Stasi. He was born with a birth defect that caused him to limp. The lack of Arian perfection must have triggered some kind of psychosis because the guy's always been more than a bit strange. After the Wall came down, he came over to the Americans. The guy is a combination of Timothy Leary and Josef Mengele. Most people thought he was dead, but about a year ago, a rumour started that he re-emerged running a clandestine MK Ultra style programme called *Lucy's Breath*. The designation is a combination of the street names for LSD and scopolamine: Lucy In The Sky and Devil's Breath."

I thank Klein for all his help and remind him to get rid of any record of his testing. There wasn't anything else I could do in Toronto. Roger was still in Washington, but even if he was here, I'm not sure I would tell him what I found.

Roger is a pompous ass, but he is smart, experienced, and bureaucratically adept. The problem is, he may also be a foreign agent, or maybe, he's working some covert counterintelligence angle for our own Section Nine.

If he's working for our agency, the hard asses in Section Nine would have no problem setting me up as the patsy in case things go sideways. Intelligence is a messy business, and if the stakes are high enough, even my own people won't have any problem in hanging me out to dry. Britain and the rest of the Western alliance could not afford to have the Yanks compromised. Whatever was going on, the answers would be in Washington, and that was where I had to be, but before doing anything, I need to protect myself.

I leave my dungeon headquarters and head for the Passport Control Office on the second floor. I enter to find a rather nondescript looking young man in black plastic glasses and an argyle sweater typing away on his computer.

"Good afternoon"

The young man senses my presence but keeps on working, not bothering to look up. "Good afternoon. How can I help you?"

"I need Canadian, US, and British passports, birth certificates, driver's licenses, SINs, and background cover for an operation."

He sticks his hand out, still not bothering to look up from his laptop. "Authorization papers?"

There's an awkward pause as he waits for me to hand him the authorization documents. He jiggles his hand in an impatient motion demanding papers, again, not bothering to look up from his seemingly very important work. Finally, he looks up, "I'll need your authorization documents?" He seems annoyed and more than a little impatient.

"There aren't any."

The young man sighs and goes back to whatever he was doing. "No authorization. No papers."

"Why don't you call Section Nine and tell them you're terminating the BMO operation because you don't have paperwork."

I finally got the kid's attention. Of course, there is no such thing as the BMO, but I'm guessing this clerk doesn't know that.

He looks up at me with a good deal more interest. "The BMO?"

"Listen, kid, the Brass Monkey is classified, off-the-books, black ops. I shouldn't be telling you this but I understand you have to protect your ass. If there's any fallout, you tell them Roger Ames gave you the verbal authorization."

"You're Roger Ames?"

I ignore the question, figuring the kid knows Roger's name, but he's probably never met him. The agency isn't big on handing out eight-by-ten glossies of spies. And Roger, being Roger, usually has one of his minions make such requests.

"Are you going to get me the papers or do I tell Derek, in Section Nine, you're killing the op?

"Verbal authorization... I don't know... I'd like to help, but I have explicit instructions from my boss, that any such request has to be in writing."

I wave the file folder I'm holding in front of the kid's face. "Tell you what kid, I'll initial your paperwork right here in front of you. You get in trouble you show them my initials."

"I don't know Professor Ames, that really isn't proper protocol."

"What's your name, young man?"

"Aah… Philip… Philip Dickerson."

"Okay Phil, I get it. I'll tell the Section Nine boys it can't be done, but I sure wouldn't want to be you, when Derek hears about this. Good luck, kid." I turn and head for the door.

"Wait a minute, Professor… You'll initial my paperwork?"

I stop with my hand on the door and turn. "I said I would, didn't I?" I place the file folder on the kid's desk. The folder contains several passport pictures of me, several variations of the name, Harry E. Rasske, and some preliminary background information identifying Rasske as CEO of Rasske Enterprises and HER Export-Import Ltd.

"I'll pick up the package in two hours."

As I head back to my office, I get a sinking feeling in my stomach. I just did something very dangerous, career-threatening, and stupid. I was hoping the kid wasn't much of a drinker and never heard of a Brass Monkey or H. E. Rasske.

Rasske was a fictional James Bond-type character in the early 1970s, used to promote the sale of the Brass Monkey cocktail mix. The obscure advertising campaign revolved around a made-up super-spy, H. E. Rasske, and his adventures in Macau during WWII. I was betting a millennial generation that didn't know Bogart and Greenstreet, wouldn't know H. E. Rasske and the Brass Monkey Lounge in Macau.

After picking up the documents from my new pal, Philip, I head for the bank where I withdraw fifty thousand Canadian and fifty thousand US dollars. I stuff the money into a soft leather attaché case.

With my *oh-shit* kitty in-hand, I head to a UPS store around the corner from the gallery and open an addressed mailbox under the name of Harry E. Rasske. I arrive at the airport in time to place my emergency stash containing the money, passports, birth certificates, SINs, and driver's licenses in a locker.

I stick the key to the airport locker and the key to Harry Rasske's new UPS home in an envelope along with a note and address it to Mercury Collins, ℅ The Bowley Gallery. I courier the envelope to Mercury so it arrives the next day.

The following day Mercury arrives at the gallery greeted by Billy. "This arrived for you first thing this morning. It's marked "Urgent". Billy hands Mercury the envelope.

Mercury sees the handwritten "Urgent" on the face of the envelope. It looks like Harry's handwriting but the return address is from an H. E. Rasske. She opens the envelope and reads:

"Mercury - Things in 'my business' may go south so I need to make arrangements. You already have my power of attorney and authorization to access my accounts. If for some reason I don't return, use the funds as you need them to operate the gallery. If you receive a message from Holly Martins go to the airport, find the locker that matches one of the attached keys, and send the package wherever Holly Martins tells you.

The second key is to a mailbox under the name Harry Rasske. Check the box every Tuesday and Thursday. If there's a letter from Martins asking for 50 US Limes, it means I need fifty-thousand US dollars sent to my offshore bank account.

- Love Harry, P.S. Burn this letter."

Harry Goes To Washington

I land at Dulles International around four o'clock with my overnight bag in hand. As I walk through the terminal, I notice a familiar face leaning provocatively against one of those large advertising screens promoting the new hit television series, *Modesty Blaise*. I couldn't help but smile.

Harriet kisses me on the cheek and takes me by the arm. "I've been wondering when you'd show up. Have you connected all the dots yet?"

"I've assembled a few, but the question remains, how do we stop it from happening?"

"I don't know if we can, Harry. We're kind of on our own, and as you well know, we don't even know who's on our side, or if our side is on our side. We make a cock-up of this business, and we both could go down for the count."

We remain silent as we head for the car rental. Finally, Harriet speaks, "You know, Roger is running around Washington, but who knows what that priggish twat is up to? Probably nothing good as you've always suspected." She pulls me closer, "Don't worry, Harry, we're a team, you and I, a very good one, I think."

Harriet lays back as usual while I rent a late model Mustang. She slips into the car with her usual sensual grace. I've missed her even more than I thought.

"I've missed you too, Harry."

"Still reading my mind, I see."

She laughs. "Well, if as you suspect, I'm merely a faulty connection in your noggin, then, of course, I know what you're thinking, but if truth be told, Harry, my love, you are more than a little transparent, especially when it comes to me."

She reaches across the stick shift and touches my arm. A chill runs through my body. She laughs. "Coffee. Let's have some caffeine, perhaps that will spark some sort of strategy that will help us pull our American pals back from the ledge."

"I hear there's a nice place in Georgetown where the coffee is good, the muffins are big, and the occasional politician's wife gets killed." And so we head to the scene of the crime where Anna Marcel had her last overpriced latté.

When we arrive, Harriet takes a seat in the back while I order two overpriced coffees and a four dollar chocolate chip cookie that's big enough for a family to share. As I wait for my order, the barista busies himself making a well-dressed woman a double mocha cappuccino with an extra shot of vanilla flavouring. I use the opportunity to ask the coffee chef if he was on duty the day Marcel was shot. He tells me it was his day off.

The woman beside me who's still waiting for her thousand calorie drink taps my arm. She has a story to tell, and she's dying to tell someone, anyone, even a rogue MI6 analyst who has no business even being in the country.

"I was here that day, same time every day. It's my guilty pleasure." She pushes closer; she grabs my arm tighter than she intended. She's attractive, I can smell her expensive perfume and almost taste her pink lipstick.

She's excited, her eyes are the size of saucers. She pushes closer, her breasts press hard against my arm, she raises up on her designer pumps to get close to my ear. She whispers, "The whole thing was fishy. Those two bums weren't like any tramps I've ever seen." She releases her ever-tightening grip and locks me in her stare. She waits for my response like a lover waiting for the next embrace.

"What do you mean?"

She retightens her grip and presses hard against my body. "The police said they were vagrants; down and out alcoholics desperate for money to pay for their next bender..." she pauses, allowing me to absorb the impact of her preamble. "They were certainly supposed to look like bums with their old, dirty clothes, but they were wearing eight-hundred dollar Fendi running shoes... and their hair might have been messy, but I know a salon cut when I see one."

She releases my arm. She stands back and gives me a conspiratorial look. She's flushed. She'd been desperate to tell someone what she saw.

The barista interrupts, "Lady... your cappuccino." She ignores him and comes close to me one more time. "I told the police what I saw, but they didn't even write it down. They never even took my name as a witness. That's not normal. The whole thing stinks, if you ask me, stinks to high heaven. And anyway, who robs a coffee shop for money, that's just stupid. There was something else going on. The woman was the Attorney General's wife, for Christ's sake." She turns, takes her over-priced coffee, and leaves the shop.

After I finally get served, I walk back to our table. Harriet has a bemused look on her face.

"What? You find something amusing?"

"For a guy who seems to have a *thing* for me, you certainly do a lot of flirting, when I'm around."

"Jealous?"

"You know… I think I am. I'm getting very possessive of you, Harry, my dear, so don't you go straying too far."

"In the future, I will endeavour to keep my coffee-waiting experiences on a strictly platonic level. But my new friend told me something very interesting."

I told Harriet what I found out. She wasn't surprised. I drink my coffee and split the cookie in two to share. She ignores the chocolate chip extravaganza as well as the coffee. I look at the wasted food and then at Harriet. "That coffee and cookie cost me fifteen bucks."

"Come now, Harry, you know better than that. Ghosts don't get hungry."

"Perhaps the former Attorney General will be interested to know the robbery in the coffee shop was, in fact, a hit on his wife."

"I'll bet you a four dollar chocolate chip cookie, he already knows." I pause, but Harriet can tell I have something more to say.

"What is it, Harry? You know you can trust me."

"I've set up a false identity and a cryptonym triggering Mercury to send me papers and cash. If things go badly, I might need you to get a message to her."

"Of course Harry, I'd do anything to help you."

"I don't even know if you're real or just…"

"I'm real, Harry, very, very real."

I tell Harriet about my false identity and the Holly Martins code name. She smiles at my creative choices. We leave the coffee shop with Harriet promising to dig deeper into the recent series of misadventures that have befallen the big-shots tasked with running the country. I head back to the hotel to track-down Roger. I need to find out what trouble he is getting me into, after all, it was Roger who got me involved in this operation.

The Defence Club

The Defence Club is a traditional nineteenth-century style gentleman's club located on I Street only a few blocks from the Whitehouse. The rather ordinary three-story Italianate townhouse makes it easy for the fifty-one politically powerful members to meet without having to endure the common folk often referenced in speeches given by its members who rely on elections to maintain their power. For the most part, members of the Defence Club regard elections as an irritating nuisance and work hard to promote various initiatives that make them redundant.

The place is obviously ultra-conservative, some would say belligerently rightwing. To gain entry, one of the current fifty-one dues-paying members has to pass on to their great reward, the result of which one can only assume has periodically been hastened by the occasional over ambitious lawmaker keen on gaining quick access to the backrooms of power and influence. It would not be hard to imagine some free-thinking member, having come to a liberal epiphany, to find himself tragically trampled by a team of normally docile carriage horses, or in more modern terms, a runaway delivery van.

Although the club's membership does include a few four and five-star generals, the name, The Defence Club, bears no relation to the military, patriotism, or national security. When the club was founded in the eighteen-eighties it provided a convenient defence for its all-male members to present to their over-inquisitive wives who wondered, exactly what the hell their husbands were doing till all hours of the night. The answer, of course, was networking with other muckety-mucks in planning the nation's future, when, in fact, most could be found screwing their brains out in the rented flats of their mistresses.

Tonight, the dining room is full, but one table of high-powered conspirators is of particular interest. Seated at a large round table are beer magnate Winston Pijiu, his two sons-in-law, Vice President Leonard Bowater, defence contractor, Malcolm Blackburn, British Intelligence Officer Roger Ames, and mad scientist, Arno Koch, the little man with a limp.

Old man Pijiu is not happy. "What's the status of the situation?"

Blackburn: "We finally got the right Marcel painting and we're checking it now to see exactly what she's hidden under the pigment."

Pijiu directs his attention to Roger, "Your man, this Harry fellow, is becoming a problem. Do we know if he found the painting's secrets?"

Blackburn interrupts. "My guys say the Indian art professor told them he hadn't had time to analyze the piece"

Pijiu thinks for a minute, "But we can't be sure, get rid of him."

Bowater objects, "Really? The guy is a nobody. Roger says he works in a broom closet and has no power or authority."

Roger: "That's right, I wouldn't worry about him. besides, I'm his boss; even if he goes over my head, the brass thinks he's nuts."

Pijiu: "I don't like it. He's a loose end. I don't understand why you got him involved?"

Roger: "Look… if things go wrong, we'll need a patsy, and he's perfect. He's not American, he's a foreign agent, he has a reputation of being crazy, and he's operating without any official cover. Besides, he's only half English; my people will have no problem cutting him loose. And, I doubt the Canadians will give a damn."

Pijiu isn't convinced, "This Harry is a smart guy. I've seen your file on him. He's like a dog with a bone. Once he gets his teeth into something, he can't let it go. Take him out."

Bowater: "I don't like the idea of killing people."

Malcolm: "Are you nuts, Arno's concoction will kill hundreds, maybe more. It will be worse than the opioid epidemic. And without a crisis, we don't have an excuse to declare martial law."

Roger: "Well... I guess we can always make Arno the patsy; he's German and crazy, and besides, he created the drug."

Arno has been sitting quietly eating; he almost chokes on a piece of steak hearing Roger offering him up as the new patsy. "Now wait just a goddam minute. If I go down, we all go down. You better not try to fuck me."

Pijiu: "Keep your lederhosen on, Arno, nobody's setting you up. This Harry will be the patsy like Roger suggests. It makes the most sense."

Malcolm: "Let's see if we can tie this Harry to the drug. Maybe we plant some evidence on his guy, Klein. He's a chemist at York University and he's working with Harry on the drug. My guys tell me he did the tests on the cognac Anna sent him."

Pijiu: "Good. It's agreed. Roger's Harry is the patsy no matter how this operation turns out. And Malcolm, tell your boys to get rid of the painting once we know its secrets."

I'm Just An Analyst

As I enter the hotel lobby, the desk clerk waves me over. He's holding a Polaroid in one hand and a sealed envelope in the other. "I believe this is for you." He hands me the envelope.

"Who left it?"

"A young Chinese woman gave me a hundred dollars to give that envelope to the man in this picture." He hands me the photograph. It's a picture of me in the coffee shop talking to the cappuccino lady. I thank the desk clerk who's disappointed the delivery of the envelope didn't result in another c-note.

The envelope contains a type-written note on expensive stationery: *"Leave the hotel, now! A limo is waiting for you out front. - A Friend."*

I stop and inspect the stationery for clues. Nothing is evident. Whoever left the note was careful to keep it simple and direct, if somewhat ominous, if not for me, perhaps for the over-friendly coffee shop witness.

I spot the limo immediately; it's parked illegally in front of the hotel with a very attractive Chinese woman leaning on the front fender while talking on her phone. She spots me, hangs up, and opens the back passenger door of the black limousine. She motions me to get in.

A well-dressed, sixty-year-old Chinese man, with a shock of expensively cut white hair, occupies the other half of the backseat.

He greets me with a broad smile, "Good afternoon Harry?"

"Is it?"

"Oh… it's a beautiful day, the sun is shining and all is right with the world… at least it will be when we conclude our business."

"Our business? I don't know who you are or who you think I am, but I doubt very much we have any business to discuss."

"You're Harry, the MI6 agent looking into Anna Marcel's premature demise."

"You are very much mistaken. I'm a lowly cultural attaché taking in the sites."

"Yes, of course, you are. Aren't we all?" He reaches into the inside breast pocket of his suit jacket and pulls out his official PRC identification. He flips open the leather ID wallet with the emblem of the People's Republic of China emblazoned on the front in gold. The identification card inside identifies the man as Yang Guozhi, Economic and Cultural Attaché.

He smiles at my reaction, "As you can see, Washington is full of attachés."

I hand him back his ID. "The woman in the photograph…"

"Don't worry about her. She's just a woman in a coffee shop, nothing to concern yourself with."

"What do you want, Mr. Yang?"

"Very good Harry, so many Americans get that wrong."

"I'm not an American."

"Yes I know, Harry. What is the expression, 'neither fish nor foul.' I find names can be very interesting, and sometimes very telling. Take mine, for instance, Guozhi, it means 'ordered government.' Interesting don't you think? And your name, Harry, there have been many interesting Harrys in our business, Harry Lime, Harry Palmer…"

"Those are both fictional characters. They're not real. And Harry Lime was a black marketeer, not a spy."

He ignores my corrections. "The British do love their spy stories, but as far as real or fantasy goes, my understanding is you have some trouble distinguishing the difference."

"I don't mean to be rude, Mr. Yang, but I did want to visit the National Gallery before it closes." I reach for the door handle but I hear a click. He grabs my arm, tighter than he intended. I give him a hard look. He releases my arm.

"Apologies Harry, sometimes I don't know my own power."

"Oh, I think you know exactly how much power you have, and how much more you want."

He smiles. "To the point then, Harry, my friend. We want you to kill Pijiu Wei." The statement is flat, lacking any emotional undertones.

I laugh out loud. "You got to be kidding? I'm not sure who you think I am or what you think I do, but I don't go around killing people."

"Of course you do, Harry. You killed that mechanic of your's, Freddy Laoshu, and his employee. And besides, don't you want to get to the bottom of that *Sister Project* business?"

"That business died with Freddy."

"Are you sure? Think about it Harry, you're the man with the imagination. Things like that don't die, they just morph and evolve into something else, something far more sinister and reckless, something, like *Lucy's Breath*." Yang spends the next fifteen minutes filling me in on the *Lucy's Breath* business and the people behind it. When he finishes, he looks at me with interest, "You don't seem surprised."

"I knew bits and pieces, but you've connected all the dots. What I don't get is why you want to stop it, you and Pijiu are both MSS."

"Harry, my friend, China is a vast and complex country with many vying interests and factions. Taking over the US government and turning America into a police state is not in the best economic interests of my country. A strong capitalistic United States means a strong consumer economy with people buying Chinese manufactured merchandise. People in police states don't buy new televisions and cell phones every year. Ideologues are dangerous, whether they are Communists, Republicans, or Democrats."

"If you want to stop this, why don't you have your people get rid of Pijiu."

"That would not be beneficial for me, my family, or for my country. It's better if someone else does it. Someone like you, Harry, a man with an imagination and a reputation."

"You mean someone whose bosses think he's crazy. Well, I'm sorry about that, but I'm not killing anybody. I'm a fucking analyst."

"If these people are successful, Canada and Great Britain will be next. And the rest of Western Europe won't be far behind. This has to stop here and now!"

There's a click. The button on the door lock jumps to attention. The attractive female assistant who's been waiting outside the entire time opens the door. I get out. Yang leans across the seat as I straighten up. "Think about it, Harry. I believe you'll decide that it's the right thing to do, and frankly my friend, you have no choice." The attractive woman closes the door and gets in the front seat. The limo disappears into traffic.

An Invitation

I make my way back to the hotel. I have no idea what I'm going to do. The only thing I know for sure is that I have no intention of murdering Winston Pijiu. If different factions of the Chinese Ministry of State Security have competing agendas, and the Enterprise Division wants Pijiu dead, it's up to them to figure out how.

Yang has plenty of reliable assets in place that can get the job done. This whole thing smells like a setup: solve the problem and point the finger at a half-Canadian, half-Brit rogue fool. Me.

I wish Harriet was here.

I came to Washington to try and stop a coup that would have international repercussions, but instead, I got myself involved in an assassination plot. How would Yang even know who I am, a lowly drudge working out of a broom closet?

And if my new pal, Phil, from the Passport Control Office, gets a bureaucratic conscious and decides to cover his ass, my way out will collapse. My only hope is that Phil sees his complicity in my scheme as a oneway ticket to Belmarsh.

The throbbing pain of Roger Ames invades my blocked sinus cavities. I place the keycard to my room in the door. The maids have cleaned and left the curtains open, perhaps to allow an MSS sniper on a neighbouring rooftop to blow my brains out.

I close the curtains denying any marksman a clear target. I flop down on the bed and close my eyes, hoping to clear my head.

Something caught my attention, something sitting on top of the minibar. Is it real, or is my imagination running wild one more time, either case wouldn't surprise me?

I open my eyes focusing on an imperfection in the ceiling. I sit up slowly, hoping that my vision is more imagination than incendiary device. My eyes shift to the minibar, on it is a bottle of Hine Antique XO Premier Cru Cognac and an envelope.

I get up and stare at the envelope for what seems like a long time. I finally gain the courage to open it. It's an invitation to an opening. The invitation is an expensive reproduction of a wild horse painted in the traditional Chinese ink wash style.

*"You are cordially invited to a private showing of
Chinese ink-and-wash paintings by
Xu Beihong (1895-1953).*

*Yang Guozhi
Economic and Cultural Attaché
The People's Republic of China."*

*Circle Gallery
Dupont Circle, Washington, DC
Saturday 9:00 PM*

Clipped to the printed invitation is a handwritten
note on plain photocopy paper:
"Look in the minibar - RA"

I reluctantly open the small fridge hoping it isn't
rigged with C4. Luckily the minibar is clean, except for the Walther PPK and a single 98 mm slug
staring me in the face. My name is neatly printed
on the bullet with some sort of black marker. I
assume Roger's extravagantly expensive fountain
pen didn't work on the brass casing.

Roger, and his pal, Yang, are setting me up as the
patsy for their joint Sino-British counter-cabal
venture. He wouldn't try to pull this off without,
at least, a wink-and-a-nod from the Vauxhall
Cross bigwigs. The message is clear, kill Pijiu at
the opening on Saturday, or use the Walther on

myself. It's apparent the agency has deemed me a liability and is cutting me loose with a final deadly last hurrah.

Today is Thursday, I have less than three days to figure this out, or I'm fucked.

Time To Kill

The phone on the bedside night-table rings, "Good morning, this is your eight-thirty wakeup call." Click. It's a prerecorded automated message. I'm old enough to remember when hotels had real people wake you up. I shower, dress, and retrieve the fully loaded Walther, as well as the single slug with my name on it. I have a hearty breakfast in the coffee shop not worrying about the calories. At this stage of the game, you never know when a meal will be your last. I figure the Circle Gallery should be opening soon and if not, maybe I can sneak in without being noticed. I take a casual walk to Dupont Circle where the gallery is located in an elegant brownstone that probably dates back to the eighteen-hundreds.

An elderly security guard stands watch, with his eyes half-closed. As I reach for the front door, I feel an ancient paw grab my shoulder. The old man is stronger and more alert than he looks, probably ex-military or police. "The gallery isn't open yet. They're still setting things up for to-morrow's big opening."

I smile in what is supposed to be a reassuring manner. "Yes, I know." I reach into the breast pocket of my suit jacket. The old man's eyes narrow and his hand moves ever so slightly to the revolver hanging from his belt. I pull out my diplomatic ID and flip it open, "I'm checking security for my boss who's invited to tomorrow's shindig. You know how these embassy types are, always worried some crackpot might throw an egg at them, or worse."

The septuagenarian rent-a-cop looks at my credentials with more than a little skepticism. "The Secret Service already checked things out early this morning."

"All I need to do is take a quick look around so I can tell my boss I did it. I'll be out of your hair lickety-split. You can call, Roger Ames, my boss, or check the guest list, he'll be on it."

The old man hands me back my ID. "Alright young man, but make it quick. And don't touch anything."

"Thanks. It's most appreciated."

"Just be quick about it."

I nod acceptance of his terms and enter the gallery. I find the room where the exhibit is taking place. Gallery workers are hanging the images. A forty-something Chinese woman yells at the workers in Mandarin. A young male assistant interprets in an equally demanding manner. I quickly scan the large rectangular space. There are exits at either end of the room leading to other galleries.

The woman turns and looks at me. She points to one of the exits. "*CHUQU!*" Her assistant doesn't need to interpret but does anyway. "GET OUT!"

I smile and bow slightly. She's not impressed. Both her and her boy-toy turn back to the poor gallery workers and continue their harassment.

There is nothing particularly unusual about the space. When the shit hits the fan, there are two exits. The one on the right is fairly close to the front door, with the one on the left leading to the back of the gallery. I decide to see where it leads. As I pass the bitchy Chinese lady, I tap her on the shoulder, she turns. I point to one of the beautiful horses framed in a simple gold leaf frame, "That one should be a little higher."

She looks me in the eye speaking in an almost violent whisper, "*Gundan!*"

I get the message and leave. I make my way through a secondary space with other Chinese horse paintings by more contemporary artists.

The room leads to a back area with offices, an emergency fire exit, and a washroom. I decide to check the facilities. The bathroom has half-a-dozen stalls. I pick the last one and enter, closing and locking the door behind me.

I stand on the toilet seat so I can reach the drop-ceiling. I push open one of the panels and place the Walther that I've wiped-clean of fingerprints in the ceiling. I put the panel back and leave. I make my way through the gallery and exit the front door waving to the elderly security guard.

I'm not sure what I've accomplished. There will probably be a metal detector put in place for the opening, so at least I have a weapon available in-case I need it. Chances are, I probably wouldn't be able to get to it before some hyper Secret Service agent puts a bullet in my brain, but at least the weapon is no longer in my possession.

A Killer Opening

The Good, The Bad, and The Ugly
"You see in this world, there are two kinds of people, my friend, those with loaded guns and those who dig." - Blondie

The phrase *dressed to kill* comes to mind. I'm not an overly vain person, but I do have to admit, the image in the mirror of a well-knotted Turnbull and Asser tie and Kilgour bespoke suit does make for a dashing figure. It would be a shame to have the outfit ruined by a 9 mm slug. Perhaps tonight, the more appropriate turn-of-phrase should be *dressed to be killed*.

I take a moment to reflect on the various scenarios that might play out at tonight's made for mayhem event. You should be aware by now, if not from this account, then from my previous lengthy regurgitation of the *Sister Project* mess, that I see my life as a mental movie with fungible scenes unspooling onto the floor of my overactive imagination.

And so the final confrontation from *The Good, The Bad, and The Ugly* repeats in a never-ending loop of alternative climaxes as if Sergio Leone couldn't decide who should be left standing.

I didn't know which character I was about to play. Was I Blondie, Tuco, or Angel Eyes? At least I had a loaded gun stashed in the ceiling of the Circle Gallery bathroom, and that is more than I can say for Tuco.

Having attained a transcendent state of heightened apprehension and divine inevitability, I leave for the gallery.

As expected, there is a metal detector installed in the entry hall with half-a-dozen Secret Service Agents and an equal number of MSS muscle patrolling the building. *Xu Beihong's* horse paintings are remarkable. I casually make the rounds inspecting each piece. I feel a woman's arm pull me close. The smell of sweet osmanthus mixed with rose honey and orange blossoms and the feel of soft fabric overwhelms my already overcharged senses. I turn my head. It's Mercury, the lovely Mercury. At last, a friendly ally wrapped in the most exotic package of black silk and gold ornamentation.

She sees the look in my eye and smiles a knowing feline smile. "I know, Harry, you don't have to say anything. I know your emotions are divided, but you'll work it out... eventually."

What is Mercury doing here? It's too dangerous.
"You can't be here. You have to leave."

"You sent me a message along with an invitation.
It wasn't something I could ignore, not if I wanted to keep you as my... boss." She hands me the
invitation she received. "Turn it over."

I flip the card over and read: *Mercury - I'm a
friend of Harry's. He needs our help. Take the airport locker key he sent you and retrieve the attaché case. Rent a car and drive to Washington.
Leave the package in the car and park across the
street from the gallery. Give Harry the keys and
tell him to leave it at the airport in longterm parking, then, get out. - Holly Martins'*

Mercury slips the keys to the car into my suit
jacket pocket. "It's a silver Civic Coupe." She sees
I'm confused, "Didn't you send me the note?"

"No... it must be Harriet."

"Whose Harriet?"

"I don't really know."

"Harry, are you alright? I'm worried about you."

"No need, I have a loaded gun hidden in the bathroom ceiling."

"A gun? I don't know what you're involved in, but it's not going to end well. You don't need to save the world. Let's just leave. We can drive home and rethink this whole thing."

"I can't. See that guy in the corner, surrounded by all the security, that's Winston Pijiu."

"Pijiu Breweries?"

"Yes. He's planning a *coup*. And over there, that's Yang Gouzhi, an MSS spook. He wants me to kill Pijiu. And over there, that's Roger Ames, my boss, watching this whole mess unfold."

"Are you fucking nuts. I'm taking you home. Come on, we're leaving. Now!"

"I don't do what they ask, I'm a dead man. Take the car and go home. Get out before it's too late."

"Where's that gun hidden?"

"Leave now or you're fired."

"Good. I'm leaving." She stomps off heading for the back of the gallery. I'm relieved. At least Mercury is safe.

Slowly, I start to circle the room heading towards the back where I can retrieve the Walther. The sound of Ennio Morricone's haunting score plays in my head. Pijiu, Yang, and Roger all seem to be watching me as I circle the room.

As I make the rounds, casually looking at the exquisite horse paintings I see in the glass, the reflection of Yang's lovely Chinese assistant mirroring my every move. Her form-fitting gold and green silk cheongsam is too tight to hide a weapon, but anything could be hidden in the matching silk clutch she's carrying. She is extremely elegantly turned-out with her jet black waist-length hair piled high on her head, held in place by an elaborate gold *fa-zan* hairpin.

I work my way to the exit that leads to the back where the Walther is hidden. I am about to head down the hall when I find myself face-to-face with Mercury. She throws her arms around me and kisses me with more passion than could be mustered by acting. "You can't fire me. I love you." She slips the Walther into my suit jacket pocket. "Now, I can leave." She kisses me one more time, in such a tender fashion, that I feel my knees buckle. "See you at home." She leaves not looking back. I watch, maybe for the last time, the beautiful Mercury as she exits the gallery. Her words linger in my head like the sweet smell of some exotic orchid.

The room goes black.

BANG! ... BANG! BANG!

There's a series of female shrieks and a burst of shouted instructions in both English and Chinese. The lights come back on. Pijiu lies dead on the floor. Blood slowly stains his crisp white shirt. Yang's assistant is by my side. She looks at me, smiles, then down at the Walther I didn't realize I was holding. She screams. "*Qiang!* Gun! He's got a gun!"

I turn and look at her. There is a sense of excitement mixed with a professional calm on her face. In a sweeping, almost balletic movement, she pulls the long elegant gold *fa-zan* from her hair and thrusts it towards my carotid. My hand holding the gun instinctively goes to block her.

The force of the contact knocks the Walther out of my hand. Several shots are fired in our direction. The hairpin has pierced my arm. The pain paralyzes me for a moment. I remove the *fa-zan* and drop it on the floor.

The woman is surprisingly strong. Her powerful fingers wrap around my neck, banging my head backward cracking the glass of one of *Xu's* paintings. I use the palm of my hand to thrust up towards her chin driving her backward, which only serves to give her MSS pals a clean shot.

Guests are running in all directions. One slug whistles past my head putting a gaping hole in one of *Xu's* horses. Yang's assistant recovers reaching for my neck one more time. Her hands find their mark but without much force. The look on her face slowly changes from deadly determination to surprise.

Harriet, who as usual, appears out of thin air. She has retrieved the beautiful assassin's *fa-zan* and plunges it deep into the Chinese beauty's neck. The three of us are wrapped in a terminal *ménage à trois* of death. The assassin looks at me for what seems a long time but it must only have been for a second.

More shots are fired; several hit the beautiful assassin who shields me from their intended target. "Harry, move!" Harriet's tone is calm but urgent. "Get to the car."

People are clambering for the exits. I manage to
make it out to the back offices in the confusion. I
follow other terrified guests out the fire exit. I
manage to find the waiting silver Civic parked
across the street from the gallery. I hear sirens.
What seemed like an endless firefight must have
only lasted a couple of minutes. I use the key fop
Mercury gave me to open the Civic. I get in, start
the car, and hit the accelerator.

I peel away from the curb and head for Dulles
Airport. There's an envelope sitting on the passenger seat with "Harry" written across the front
in Mercury's handwriting. I reach for the envelope and notice blood has stained the French cuff
of my shirt.

As the adrenalin of the incident subsides I realize
exactly how much pain I'm in. That Chinese bitch
got me good with her goddam hairpin dagger. I
open the envelope trying my best not to get
blood on whatever is inside. It's a oneway, first-
class airplane ticket to London in the name of
Harry Rasske.

When I get to the airport I park in longterm parking as per the instructions. I look in the backseat,
but the attaché case isn't there. I start to worry,
the package must be in the trunk.

I open the trunk but nothing is there. I stand and
stare at the empty boot as if staring will magical-
ly make my money and passports appear. Did
someone get to the getaway bag before I did? As
a last resort, I flip open the spare tire compart-
ment. The tire is missing, but the attaché case
and an overnight bag lie side-by-side.

I make my way to the public washrooms and find
a stall. Mercury has provided me with a complete
change of casual travelling clothes and a first aid
kit, clever girl. I manage to stem the flow of blood
with a lot of bathroom paper towels and finish
the job with a bandage from the kit.

I keep all the British IDs in the briefcase and
shove a packet of ten thousand US dollars in my
jacket pocket. The rest of the IDs and cash I put
in the overnight bag. I finish changing my clothes
and dump my expensive Savile Row suit and
blood-stained shirt in the trash. I leave the
overnight bag in an airport locker in case I need
another escape route through the States. It's still
an hour until my redeye leaves for London. I
head for the first-class lounge and try to relax.

H. E. Rasske

One Year Later

The incident at the Circle Gallery managed to
stabilize the fragile US political landscape. Vice
President Bowater ran for President without the
financial assistance of the Pijiu fortune which
suddenly seemed to evaporate overnight. I suspect Yang Gouzhi had something to do with that.
Bowater was soundly trounced in the election by
the Democratic Governor of California. Malcolm
Blackburn was indicted by the Southern District
of New York for trying to bribe the Junior Senator
from the Empire State, and Arno Koch disappeared into the rat hole from whence he came.

The attempted coup aided by the poisoning of
large numbers of US citizens with hallucinogenic
drugs was avoided. For most people, it is hard to
believe that such a scheme ever had a chance to
work, but the very attempt, if implemented,
could have caused a massive economic and public health crisis. But then, how many people in
the home of the brave and land of the free know
about the attempted Wall Street Putsch of 1933.

Americans are as delusional about their history
as they are about their place in it. America was

founded in revolution and moulded in Civil War; it is in its nature to be violent and domineering, with an inclination for isolation and self-importance, fostered by a jaundiced view of politics and a Saturday morning cartoon perspective on its past. Perhaps a more charitable view of lawmakers would attract a better breed of participants, then again, perhaps not.

The Americans may not have liked paying taxes to the Crown, and for that matter still, don't like paying taxes to their own Government no matter how many services it provides. But the fact is, the countries that grew out of the British Empire and follow the parliamentary model have had stable democratic rule without the weekly mass murders by gun-toting extremists suffering from delusions of victimization that appear regularly on the evening news.

I will say this, despite its faults, the United States is resilient; it survives, and I suppose, in the final analysis, survival is the objective, and that goal was achieved, both for the Americans and for me, albeit in the slightly altered guise of my new alter-ego, H. E. Rasske.

I've managed to re-establish myself in a large loft in a building next to the former Shoreditch High Street Iron Works. The building was being converted into a fashionable restaurant and art gallery complex with studios and apartments above, but the developer ran out of funds. He was more than happy to accept my financial assistance and take me in as a partner with the condition the top floor was mine.

Life has settled into a quiet, bordering on boring, existence. I did grow a beard; not so much as a disguise, but more of a change of pace rather than a change of face.

I miss Mercury and Harriet and both are constantly in my thoughts. Every morning I take a short walk down the street to a shabby little dive that serves great coffee and a rather nice cheese omelette. I understand, a man on the run should not form such easily discovered routines, but perhaps, I'm hoping to be discovered, if for no other reason than to increase my heartbeat which seems to miss the adrenalin rush. I take the last bite of toast and drain the coffee from its mug when a familiar face appears at my table.

"Well... hello dear boy. How have you been?" Roger sits down opposite me. The owner of the café brings Roger a mug and fills it with coffee until it overflows onto the napkin underneath.

"You found me?" I know, it's a stupid thing to say, obviously he's found me.

"You didn't try very hard to hide, old sport. Your partner in miss-direction, Philip, folded like an old suitcase without even the threat of water-boarding or other more persuasive techniques."

"What do you want, Roger?"

"I'm here to offer you a job?"

"A job? You want me back in the Circus?"

Roger smiles, "That ship has sailed, my boy, this is more of a stringer's role, an outside contractor, doing things unofficially; things that require discretion and deniability."

"In other words, I'd be on my own."

"That's correct."

"Hung out to dry."

"Exactly."

"Fuck you."

Roger smiles at my response. "You still have a way with words, old friend. He takes his extravagant Graf von Faber-Castell fountain pen out of his sports coat and prints an address on the napkin in front of him.

"What's this?"

"An address."

"What am I supposed to do with it?"

"You are supposed to kill the person who currently occupies the flat on the third floor."

"You're crazy. I'm not a killer. I didn't kill Pijiu for Yang and I'm not going to kill whoever lives at..." I pause to look at the address. It's been obliterated by the spilled coffee. I hand it back to Roger.

 "I can't read it. It's blurred"

He takes back the napkin and starts to rewrite the address, but the napkin is beyond its ability to accept ink from a fountain pen. I take the pen out of his hand.

"I told you, I'm not a killer."

"Do I need to remind you about, Freddy, your mechanic, and his sidekick, two murders you tried to pin on me?"

"It got you the job on the top floor."

"Actually, I'm back home now with a new promotion for my handling of the *Lucy's Breath* affair."

It figures. Roger is like a cockroach, you just can't get rid of the fucker. I was in a bind. The FBI still had me on a list of suspects for the murder of Winston Pijiu. They weren't too inclined to look very hard since they knew it wasn't me, but if the British decided to give me up, they would have no choice but to pin the killing on me.

"Who killed Pijiu?"

"Probably, one of Yang's people. You were just the patsy, but I had confidence you'd manage to wriggle out of it somehow."

"Making me the patsy... that was your idea?"

"Brilliant, don't you think?"

"Fuck you."

"You're repeating yourself, old friend. And anyway, you did try to set me up for Freddy and friend, but luckily, it worked out in my favour."

"What's the address?"

"12 Barry Road, East Dulwich."

I write the address in a notebook I carry in my jacket pocket. "So who lives there?"

"Arno Koch."

"Jesus… what the hell is that Nazi doing here?"

"Just because the Chinese didn't get away with *Lucy's Breath* in the States doesn't mean they won't try it here. We suspect he and his friends in the MSS are trying to set it up now."

"Tell me, does this job pay?"

"You mean for the love of country, isn't compensation enough?"

"You want me to be an outside contractor, I have no choice but to act like one. I want my record cleared here, in the States, and with Interpol if they're looking for me. I want H. E. Rasske officially legitimized. And I want appropriate compensation commensurate with the ask. And murder is a big, fucking ask."

Roger pauses like he's thinking it over, but I know how he works. He's already authorized to give me anything reasonable. "Alright, Harry, I can do that."

"You'll also have to pay for my expenses."

"Done, just keep receipts."

"Sure Roger, receipts for a murder, no problem. And, I'm keeping your fucking pen." I stick the pen in my jacket pocket along with the notebook and address.

"One more thing, Harry. Koch did some renovations to the third floor flat he occupies including a new picture window that overlooks the flagstone patio and garden below. We installed the new window. If someone… say someone with a bad leg and severe limp accidentally stumbled into that window, it might just give way causing that poor soul to fall to his untimely end."

"You think of everything, don't you, Roger."

"It's my job, Harry."

The Defenestration of Arno Koch

I look at myself in the shop window. Who is Harry Rasske? A hero, a servant of the Crown, a fool, or just an ordinary murderer? What happened to the old Harry? I barely recognize this new version. The neatly trimmed beard, slightly greying at the edges, hides the facade that used to be the original version. This model has all the mannerisms and attitudes of the old Harry, but I'm about to become a contract killer.

Yeah, I know I killed fucking Freddy; everybody wants to constantly remind me of that fact, but that was different or was it? Perhaps I'm as delusional and mad as Roger makes me out to be. I still haven't rationalized if Harriet exists or not. She seems to have vanished with the cancellation of the *Modesty Blaise* television series. Will the killing of Arno Koch be my undoing? Is this Roger's final retribution for me setting him up for Freddy's murder? Is this the end of my movie or just a cliffhanger to coax you to follow me one more time? Only time will tell.

I sit in the darkness of Koch's parlour. The chair is old and frayed and cheap, but I have to admit, very comfortable. It rocks back and forth in sync to my understandable nervousness. A Glock 17 rests on the arm of the heavily upholstered rocker. Shooting him would be messy and not in my brief, but people about to be murdered by defenestration generally need some persuasion; a Glock 17 seems to be a convincing persuader.

You are probably wondering how I got into the apartment since you may remember in my last memorandum involving the *Sister Project* that Harriet gave me a hard time for not knowing how to pick a lock. If you haven't read it, you should; it does provide valuable insight into the game being played and the pawns left on the board. Since then, I have learned how to pick a lock. You can learn almost anything on the Internet.

I hear someone enter the flat. The sound of the awkward shuffling of a damaged limb signals it's Arno Koch. Instead of turning on a light, he slowly makes his way to the window.

It's strange the things that flash through your head before you commit a murder; I would never open the curtain as the sunlight pouring in from the large picture window would damage my collection of abstract canvases still residing in my Toronto loft. Koch drags open one side of the thick fabric drapes. He pauses as if to catch his breath from the exertion. He drags the other side open, raising his hand to shield his eyes from the bright midday sun. He turns. The intense light must have blinded him for a moment because he doesn't see me.

"Hello, Arno."

"You're Roger's man…"

"That's right, Arno, I'm Roger's pet patsy."

"I never thought they should make you the patsy. I fought against it." He's lying, of course, but why stop him from making his case for mercy. It's the least I could do. "It was Roger, he's the one that wanted it to be you. He's the one that you should go after." He's not altogether wrong. "I'm like you, Harry, just trying to survive."

I stand. The Glock still sits on the arm of the chair. "I have to disagree, Arno, I'm not like you. I only kill people one at a time. Mass murder isn't my thing."

I can see the fear in his eyes. He lunges toward me. I react. I hit him hard with a right. He falls backward into the glass. The window makes a creaking sound as Arno slides down the glass.

He struggles to his feet. He eyes the Glock still sitting on the arm of the chair. He tries to grab it.

I catch him before he can reach it. I swing him
around flinging him into the window.

This time I can see the large picture window
start to come away from the frame but it manages to stay in place. I'll have to speak to Roger
about his people's preparation.

Koch manages to get to his feet. Fear has turned
to rage. He makes one last violent attempt to
come at me. I grab him by the lapels of his cor-
duroy jacket and swing him around so hard he is
lifted off the floor. He hits the window hard. It
gives way. Arno Koch hits the flagstone patio in a
splash of shattered glass. He is dead. H. E. Rasske
is officially a killer.

I take Roger's fancy pen from the inside pocket of
my jacket. I consider leaving it behind as I did
once before, but will it really make Roger the fall
guy for this messy cleanup? Everyone keeps
telling me; just because something doesn't work
the first time, maybe it will work the next. But,
making trouble for Roger may not be the best
thing for my future.

The time may come when things will change, but
for now, the best thing to do is to let things be.

Give Roger time to clear my legal issues and legit-
imize my new Rasske identity. As far as the new
job is concerned, why not?

I put the Graf von Faber-Castell in my pocket. It is
a nice pen. I leave Koch's flat and head for a
drink. Maybe the bartender knows how to make
a Brass Monkey. I think I'll give Mercury a call.

The End

DECEPTION
"I CANNOT FORECAST TO YOU THE ACTION OF RUSSIA. IT IS A RIDDLE, WRAPPED IN A MYSTERY, INSIDE AN ENIGMA; BUT PERHAPS THERE IS A KEY. THAT KEY IS RUSSIAN NATIONAL INTEREST."
- WINSTON CHURCHILL
WRITTEN BY JERRY BADER
ILLUSTRATED BY PAOLA CECCANTONI

DECEPTION

Deception

The world is a dangerous place, and every country has men and women tasked to protect it. These people go by many names: secret agent, intelligence officer, and analyst are just a few. Harry is one such person. He is an analyst. He spends his time reading, researching, and analyzing, followed by writing reports that often never see the light of day.

Harry is well educated with a seemingly important job, but Harry is bored. Bored, because analysts never get to be the hero, never get to order cocktails stirred not shaken, and, never, never, get the girl. Harry is frustrated, frustrated because his superiors told him the report he just spent six months working on is to be tabled, and no, he can't have a field operative to work with to follow up.

Harry has one very dangerous character flaw, he has an imagination, not something the men on the Top Floor appreciate. Harry needs to prove himself; he needs some excitement in his life, and that excitement comes in a deadly package of intrigue and murder that combines something called the *Sister Project* with a Russian master spy, H, K. Kyrsa, code name, the *Beautiful Rat*, and the devastatingly gorgeous Harriet. The question is, is it all just happening in Harry's head, or is there a real plot that needs to be stopped? Is Harry just plain crazy, or are the Russians out to mess with the West one more time? Harry is on his own, not sure who to trust. Are there any good guys in the world of espionage? The only way to find out is to find Kyrsa, the Beautiful Rat. Join Harry in his search for what may not even be real.

THE OUTLAW RIDER

The Outlaw Rider
"If you're not prepared to cheat,
you're not prepared to win."

Jesse James, the daughter of a deceased mob-connected rug salesman, becomes a jockey working for the *Hong Mian* triad in order to feed winners to State Senator Samuel Somersby. The Senator is responsible for approving California gaming licenses. To date, only Native CANGV casinos are allowed to have slots. California horse racing will die if they aren't allowed to add slot machines to their venues. Benson Yeung, Dragon Head of the *Hong Mian* triad, and his chief lieutenant, Johnny Luck, have a plan to force Somersby to approve their Native partner's demands for off-reservation gaming licenses. At the center of the plan is a unique white thoroughbred Spirit horse, prized by Native people, appropriately named Medicine Hat.

Dead End
There Are No Good Guys

It all started five years earlier with the murder of Peter Pretty Boy Chen, a low-level soldier for Benson Yeung's Hong Mian triad. Rumor had it that the Guan Yu statue that sat on the old man's desk, the symbol of his Dragon Head status as leader of the Hong Mian, was filled with priceless Pigeon Blood rubies, or at least that's what Peter Pretty Boy Chen thought. Whether he was right or wrong is a tale for another time and another place.

What's significant is, his desire to get his hands on those rubies led to his brains being splattered all over the wall of the Green Dragon Restaurant. Like all classic California mysteries the past is never forgotten or forgiven; it always comes back to raise its ugly head.

DEAD END

Fast forward five years. We first met Jesse James and her associates in *The Outlaw Rider*, when she was a young female jockey making a name for herself on the track and off under the guidance of her mentor, triad big shot, Johnny Luck. Jesse has moved up the Hong Mian ladder and has made herself a major triad player, but the past is never so far behind that it doesn't affect the present. And so *Dead End* begins.

Palermo
A Place To Die

The race took place in picturesque Palermo, Sicily, but this wasn't your typical horse race with rules designed to protect the horses, jockeys, and bettors; this was a Mafia sponsored street race: a blood sport free-for-all more suited for the Coliseum than the backstreets of the scenic Sicilian town. Race promoter, Santos Luzzato, nephew to Nicky The Mushroom Fungo, wanted in on his American Uncle's horse racing connections with the LA triads. The race leads to a series of decisions that end with a suspicious car accident that kills billionaire heiress and racehorse owner, Josephine Somersby Murphy, sister to the Governor of California, Samuel Somersby, a man with Presidential ambitions and ties to Johnny Luck, LA triad big shot.

Love, sex, murder, and racehorses create a toxic mix of intrigue and suspense that drives Luck's protégé, Jesse James, to Sicily, Argentina, England, and Switzerland in her pursuit of the truth. Who killed Josephine Murphy? Was it Luzzato, Nicky Fungo, Murphy's brother, the Governor, or was it someone closer to Jesse.

Palermo, a place to die.

PALERMO

Stone Cold
Between a Stone and a Hard Place

On the surface, Major William Stone (Retired) is merely a rich, English expatriate with a diverse military and financial services background now living in Palermo, Argentina where he runs a small art gallery along with his assistant Margarita Cervantes.

If you scratch the surface, you'll find that Stone was recently the chauffeur for Mrs. Josephine Murphy, heiress to the Murphy Peanut Butter Company, the largest peanut butter manufacturer in the USA, and owner of numerous expensive thoroughbred racehorses. This seemingly incongruous set of circumstances gets even more intriguing when you learn that Stone inherited over one billion dollars when Josephine Murphy died in a tragic, and somewhat questionable, car accident in the hills of Palermo, Sicily leaving Major Stone the bulk of her estate.

After the Murphy estate is settled, Stone disappears to reemerge in Argentina leading a quiet and peaceful life as a wealthy art gallery owner and financier. His good fortune is tempered by the fact he left the love of his life, Jesse James, protégé to gangster Johnny Luck, back in LA.

The problem is, Major William Stone died in the Falkland Islands and the man now assuming his modified identity is disgraced MI6 financial wizard Jacob Conrad. Conrad took the fall for his Vauxhall Cross masters' illegal shenanigans ending up in jail with a lengthy prison term. According to the British newspaper reports, Conrad died in Belmarsh Prison, only to be resurrected by Section Six's cyber boffins as William Stone, international financial consultant living in Hong Kong, where he runs into Charlie Long,

Dragon Head of the Wan Chai and a major rival of the Hong Mian, led by Benson Yeung and Johnny Luck.

Stone Cold dives deep into the back-story of how Jacob Conrad becomes William Stone, why he disappeared leaving Jesse behind, and who'll control the flow of cocaine into the USA. From Hong Kong to Palermo, London, Cacaloxuchitl, Mexico and Los Angeles, this is a tale of secret agents, drug dealers, money launders, and murders, all wrapped in a delicious recipe of greed, envy, cocaine, and peanut butter chili.

The Aussie Switch
Published By MRPwebmedia

Horse trainers, Davey and Pauly Cisco are looking for a fresh start in Southern California after wearing out their welcome in their native Australia. The Cisco twins are identical in looks but not personality; Pauly, like most horse trainers, pushes the envelope of acceptable practice, while his look-alike brother rips through regulations with regularity and abandon. It didn't take long for the two brothers to hook-up with a couple of conmen: an expert computer hacker who likes e-gaming and a shyster stock promoter on the lookout for eager marks willing to blow their fortunes on a shady horse-betting consortium. The one thing they didn't count on is an associate of Benson Yeung's Hong Mian triad; an ex-South Korean Colonel who operates a crooked international gambling empire. Two corrupt confidence men, unethical twin horse trainers, and doppelgänger thoroughbreds add up to a combustible confluence of confusion, miss-direction, and murder, with tentacles that twist their way through LA, Sidney, Hong Kong, Seoul, and Macau.

STONE COLD

Ballet of Bullets
The Game Is Dodging Death
Published By MRPwebmedia

Internet gambling and the expansion of casinos beyond the Nevada State Line have put a financial strain on racetracks. Johnny Luck, Hong Mian triad big shot, and his beautiful blonde ex-jockey protege, Jesse James, are always on the lookout for ways to expand the triad's gambling operation. Back in the fifties and sixties, Jai Alai was a big deal in Florida. Gamblers would fill the *frontons* and drop thousands of dollars betting on Basque athletics competing in a sport that was so dangerous it was referred to as the Ballet of Bullets and The Game Is Dodging Death.

Johnny Luck sees the potential revenue that could be produced by resurrecting the all but dead blood sport. The question is, how to make it popular again? Jesse has the answer. Television. People will bet on anything; they will also watch anything, as witnessed by the plethora of cooking shows that feature ordinary people competing for who can fry the best egg.

If there's a competition, people will bet on who will win. But where there is money, there is corruption; enter the Miami Bettor's Club, run by old Hong Mian rivals Tommy The King Kong and Marco Antonia Suarez, nicknamed *El Astronauta*. In the end, the Ballet of Bullets becomes all too real for the people fighting for control of the gambling revenue generated by the International Jai Alai League.

THE AUSSIE SWITCH

What's Your Poison?
How Cocktail's Got Their Names
Published By MRPwebmedia

Why do we call mixed alcohol drinks "cocktails"? How do they get their exotic names: names like the Singapore Sling, Screw Driver, the Alamagoozlum, the Angel's Kiss, the Hanky Panky, the Harvey Wallbanger, Sex On The Beach, the Monkey Gland, the Brass Monkey, the Margarita, the Japalac, the Lion's Tail, and many, many more? Who makes up these names, where are they invented, why, and how do you make them? These questions will be answered in "*What's Your Poison?*" by exploring the incidents, people, and places that prompted the creation of these exotic concoctions.

Organized Crime Queens
The Secret World of Female Gangsters

From the bizarre world of female Japanese motorcycle gangs to the historic rise and fall of London's Forty Elephants, the history of female organized crime is both fascinating and strange. These are the stories, both true and legendary of the female crime bosses that broke the mould of feminine gentility. This is The Secret World of Female Gangsters.

Cowboys, Lawmen, & Outlaws

When we think of the Old West, it seems like ancient history, but historically it was yesterday. Many of the characters of the post Civil War Old West lived well into the twentieth century: Bat Masterson died in 1921 and Wyatt Earp didn't pass-on until 1929. Josie Bassett, one of the Wild Bunch girls managed to hang-on until 1963 and she only died then because

BALLET OF BULLETS

she got kicked in the head by a horse.

History doesn't end with an era, remnants, artifacts, and people overlap. History doesn't stop because technology and style move on.

The future is more likely to look like the film *Brazil* with its jury-rigged conglomeration of antique flotsam and modern-day technological jetsam, than the bright shiny newness of *Star Trek*. Turning history into fantasy is dangerous; it leads to mistaken notions and bad decisions. Maybe it's time to grow up and see the heroes of the Old West, as they really were, cowboys, lawmen, and outlaws.